The Better Monster

K.L Hart

Published by K.L Hart, 2022.

This is a work of fiction. Similarities to real people, places, or events are entirely coincidental.

THE BETTER MONSTER

First edition. October 20, 2022.

Copyright © 2022 K.L Hart.

Written by K.L Hart.

The Better Monster

K.L Hart

Published by K.L Hart, 2022.

This is a work of fiction. Similarities to real people, places, or events are entirely coincidental.

THE BETTER MONSTER

First edition. October 20, 2022.

Copyright © 2022 K.L Hart.

Written by K.L Hart.

For Mum,

Who only reads this page to make sure the dedication is to her.

Play smart not hard right mum :)

Chapter One

"Miss, is this available in a size six?" The lady holding a cream duster jacket asks me, I plaster the customer service smile on my face,

"Sorry we don't have it in stock, but I can order it in for you, it will arrive on Wednesday." I reply sweetly.

"Perfect, would you like me to pay now?" She reaches around her to grab her purse out of her bag

"No, no you can pay on collection, can you leave your name and number and we can give you a call when it's ready to collect."

"Of course." She comes over to the counter and gives me her details. I wonder over to the stool as the customer leaves and grind my teeth when the expected sharp pain goes through my side, I sigh as I look around at all the nice clothes and accessories neatly positioned around the small shop, I used to have dreams and ambitions, but this is all I have to look forward to in life, minimum wage selling gorgeous shit I can never actually buy and pretending that I have a normal happy life. My dreams of travelling the world and doing something worthwhile will never come to fruition even though I worked hard at school and got the best results from all my exams but it was all for nothing. My parents disowned me four years ago and refuse to even acknowledge my existence, the only person I have left to count on is Millie, she is my ride or die and I don't think I would have made it to twenty-one without her.

"Skye, can you do inventory on the new stock out back?" My boss Lucy asks, and I nod my head heading to the back room where boxes are piled in the corner. I open each box, count the items, and check them off the list, great use of my brain cells this is. I know I am in a foul mood; I am most days but that's what happens when you are miserable with your life. When I finish the inventory, I put my hand behind one of the racking's and pull out my secret stash, I sneak out the back and flick the lighter using the orange flame to light the cigarette, I am not a heavy smoker and only really smoke one or two while I am at work but it takes the edge off, it calms my nerves at the end of the day. I look to the sky which has suddenly darkened as a rain drop falls on my nose, London in October means rain and a lot of it, I rush the rest of my cig, so I don't get caught when the heavens open fully and make it inside more or less dry.

"Fifteen minutes then we can all go home and enjoy our Friday night." Lucy says with a grin as I walk back onto the shop floor. I smile back, it's fake but I've perfected it so much it's hard to tell. Ugh I need to shake this mood off, tonight's going to be a good night after all, he promised as much!

I walk into the little flat in Peckham and kick my shoes off in the hallway, my gaze skims over the three doors that lead to a small bedroom, a minute bathroom and a cramped kitchen – living room, I can see the pain peeling and the cracks throughout the walls, cleaning this place every day will not take away from the fact it's crumbling.

"Good your back! I am off out with the boys." I glare at Jay as he appears from the living room,

"I thought you were taking me out tonight?" His mouth curves up in a lazy smirk but his eyes tell me what's coming.

"Why the fuck would you think that? Your nothing but an embarrassment." He stalks towards me and I flinch, "All your good for is sucking cock and you're not winning any prizes there either!" He shoves my shoulder, "Look at you, who would ever want you, I question why I put up with your skanky arse all day every day." He sneers in my face; he shoves me again and I feel the cold wall at my back. I look up at him, he is a good-looking guy with his stylish black hair, his big brown eyes that are a lighter colour when he's not mad and his perfectly symmetrical face but I can no longer see past the ugliness that shows through from within him.

"Why don't you leave then!" I snap and I regret it instantly, fuck why do I never learn, just stay still and stay quiet.

"Oh, I am not leaving, if anyone will leave it's you, you fucking whore!" The first hit lands in my gut winding me in an instant, I bend over clutching my belly, he yanks my hair so I am upright again and he leans in close, "But good luck trying to leave, bitch!" He punches me again and I crumple to the floor, I feel the warm streaks of tears stream down my cheeks. I watch his retreat from me but I know to stay still and not make any noise, I hear the rustling of his jacket and the spray of his aftershave before he makes his way back to me. "Tidy this shit hole up and sort yourself out, I'll be back when I feel like dealing with you!" He kicks me hard in the side and I cry out in pain, I hear him laugh as he leaves the flat. I let out all my tears and as quick as they came, I wipe them away locking all that crap away and pushing it do the depths of my soul. The pain is worse when I first move to stand gripping the wall to help steady myself, the new bruises are directly on top of old ones and nothing I haven't pretended wasn't there before. I slowly walk into the bathroom and grab the numbing cream from out of the cabinet, I slather over the black, blue and purple colours that make up the expanse my back my sides and my belly, I used to wish he wouldn't do it now I wish he would do it somewhere I couldn't hide. I sit on the couch and put the tv on, my phone rings and I grab it off the coffee table a smile spreads on my face when Millie pops up on the screen.

"Hello," I answer,

"So where is he taking you?" She asks, I let out a sigh,

"Nowhere, he's gone out and left me here."

"You have got to be fucking with me."

"Nope I think he forgot."

"Well fuck that, get ready I am on my way, we are going out! Do you have a dress?"

"Er, I don't think that's such a good idea."

"No, it is! Show the prick you won't be left in the house while he does what he likes!"

"I don't even have any money!"

"Don't worry about it, I'll bring the dress, makeup, money and pre drinks just get in the shower." She hangs up before I can protest again. Fuck! My hand hovers over the button to call Millie back, what are my options? I get a beating for going out? I get a beating for not looking good enough, for being asleep when he gets back, if I am honest with myself there doesn't need a reason for him to raise his fists. He normally doesn't even come home the same night so he might not even know that I've had a night of fun. Fuck it, worst case scenario he finally kills me but then at least I would be free. Excitement courses through me as I grab some pain killers then jump in the shower.

By the time I am washed and wrapped in a towel the doorbell rings and I swing it open to find my best friend in her pyjamas with a suitcase.

"You moving in?" I ask her eyeing the suitcase she's ogling behind her she as she walks past me and into the front room.

"We need supplies, here are the supplies!" She opens the suitcase pulls out a bottle of Vodka and a few cans of Red Bull. "Get the glasses then!" I rush to the kitchen and grab the glasses as Millie cranks up the volume on the TV putting the music channel on. Millie shows me dress after dress and I point at the only one that doesn't have a low back or cut outs in the sides. She throws the red dress at me and starts unloading her make-up onto the coffee table, she beckons for me to sit on the floor in front of her, so I do,

"I can't believe he just left you on your birthday, your twenty-first birthday too, why are you still with him?" She says as she taps my face with the beauty blender,

"It's complicated," I admit, it's true, I don't want to be here with him, but what choice do I have? How am I meant to leave?

"Complicated or not, you deserve better." She states matter of factly, I shrug one shoulder and like that the conversation is dropped.

"So, how's the job at the paper going?" I ask,

"You mean the internship from hell?" She rolls her eyes as she swipes liquid lipstick on my bottom lip, "They treat me like I am some sort of idiot that's only good for fetching their lunches, four years I have spent in college studying PR, Advertising, Communication and Journalism and they won't even hear me out! I am ready to look for something else, I wanted to be a journalist but I am not putting up with that, I have been in discussions with an agency about becoming a PR specialist for some of their social media influencer's which sounds very promising!"

"Oooh, fancy!" I reply with a grin. It takes Millie a hot minute to finish my hair and makeup but when she is done, and I have my dress on I have to do a double take in the mirror. My Auburn hair reaches my lower back and the thick curls have been eradicated of all frizz and look bouncy and shiny. My make-up has been done to perfection, I am perfectly contoured and my light blue eyes are dusted with browns and golds with a winged liner. My Lips are the same deep red as my dress, the dress itself fits me like a glove and shows off the little curves I have, the lace sleeves cover my arms and it comes to mid-thigh, showing off my legs which look longer than usual in the tall heels I have on.

I walk back into the living room where Millie is now looking like the goddess, she is in her very short black dress with the low v neck which accentuates her very slim figure, her golden hair is sleek straight and her smoky black eyes make her green eyes pop. She downs the rest of her drink and grabs her clutch,

"Ready?" She asks and I nod grabbing my little bag and putting the chain on my shoulder, we exit the flat and head outside.

"It's so cold!" I say with a shiver,

"It won't be when we are in the club." She grins at me as she walks towards the taxi and hops in, I slide in next to her and shut the door, Millie tells the driver where we want to go and then she scrolls on her phone. One thing I have always hated about going out is you can't take a jacket or a coat, it's like an unspoken law around here, even when the weather is below zero and it's pissing it down with rain us girls will brave it on a night out.

"Ok, you need to promise you will have fun tonight!" Millie tells me and I chuckle,

"I Promise!"

Chapter Two

Millie hooks her arm in mine and we smile at the two bouncers who let us straight in the building, we can feel of the bass from across the street and the music gets louder in my ears with every step. Once we go through the set of double doors we step into the crowd of people, Everyone's dancing and mingling and the coloured lights bounce off them as they move around the space. We make our way through the crowd to the bar; Millie orders our drinks while I start bopping to a remix of Ladbroke Grove by AJ Tracey.

"Here!" Millie shouts in my ear and I turn to see four shots on the bar with our two actual drinks. Millie picks one up and nods her head for me to do the same and I do as I am told. "To girls' night!" She shouts and we both knock one shot back, my face screws up as it burns down my throat,

"Sambuca, really?" I roll my eyes at her and she chuckles, we pick up the next shot and do that one too, my face screws up even more, Ugh Tequila. I wash the shots down with some of my Archers and Coke and I can feel a slight buzz from the shots already. I grab Millie's hand and lead her into the centre of the dance floor and start dancing with her, were both full of smiles and giggles, I can honestly say I didn't know what I was missing, for one night I couldn't care less what's waiting for me at home, and I actually let myself have some fun! After three or four songs I need another drink, I lean into Millie and shout in her ear,

"Drink?" Millie nods and we weave through the crowd and go back to the bar. We order drinks and when they arrive, we do the shots in quick succession and grab our drinks, leaning against the bar we watch the room. The buzz of the alcohol intensifies and I get the craving I always get when I drink,

"Millie, do you have any cigs?"

"What is it with you and drunk smoking?" She asks on a chuckle and pulls a pack out of her bag along with a lighter. "I came prepared for your strange ways!" She teases as she hands me them.

"You coming?" I ask and she shakes her head,

"Nah, I'll wait here for you." I turn and walk through the club to find the Smoking area, I see the back door and head for it, Just as I get near it, I spot someone I really did not want to see, I carry on walking as I know he has seen me already and I ball my hands into fists as I walk past Jay and his friends, the girl who is wearing no more than a bikini grinding on Jay's lap doesn't notice the glare he is sending in my direction. Fuck this shit! I stop momentarily and smile sweetly at my boyfriend and then give him the middle finger before flipping my hair and continuing walking to the smoking area. I walk to the far end of the outdoor space and take a seat under one of the heaters, I take the packaging of the cigarettes get one out and light it, I relax a bit as soon as I take a deep lungful of smoke and nicotine and focus on savouring the feeling. I have to get out, tonight! I am going to go back into the club tell Millie everything and ask her to help me leave the piece of shit before he even leaves the club! Well, that's what I always think I would do but after the last time can I risk it? Can I risk Millie, I shake my head when I look up from my lap I see a hot as hell guy in a suit barely contains his muscles, I swear I can see every contour of his upper body and my body reacts at the sight of him walking towards me, for some reason my eyes are transfixed on the tall, dark and handsome guy who looks so out of place here, I know I am staring, he knows I am staring, but I just can't look away. He takes a seat next to me and I don't even question why, I just continue staring at him.

"Can I steal one of those?" The guy asks in his American accent, he points at the cigarettes in my hand and I pass him the box, I examine his face and I don't think I've ever seen a guy who remotely compares, from his brooding eyes that are the colour of liquid emeralds to his chiselled features all the way to his tanned skin and perfect nose, that's not including the sexy as sin five o'clock shadow, he takes one of the cig's and puts it to his full plump lips and lights it, he looks ahead and I can see his strong jawline tick. I continue my assessment of him, his dark brown hair is perfectly styled in a fashionable short blowout that's pushed back casually with tapered sides and back. He turns to face me and our eyes connect and I feel like I couldn't look away, especially when one side of his mouth curves up and a dimple appears, Jesus this man was something else.

"What's a pretty girl like you sitting out here on her own?" He asks his voice deep,

"Just getting some nicotine." I say copying his small smile,

"I see, how's your night going?" I shrug,

"Not bad, considering my prick of a boyfriend ditched me on my birthday and then I find him here with some other girl grinding on him." Ugh why did I just blurt all of that out?

"The guy sounds like a moron!" He looks back into the smoking area. We both continue to smoke in silence, I stub my fag butt in the bucket of sand and stand,

"Well see ya," I say as I start to walk away, the guy grabs my wrist and I spin, I have to look up to see his face now he's standing and I swallow hard, the tingles going up my arm from where he is touching me making me all hot. He leans down so his lips are near my ear.

"You deserve so much better! Remember that." He kisses me on the cheek before releasing me and walking around me, disappearing back into the club. I stand frozen for a second and then my fingers trace over my cheek where the strange sensation is still fluttering on my skin. I shake my head and force myself out of my daze. I take a deep breath before walking back in, I need to find Millie.

I search everywhere for Millie but I can't find her, I weave through the dance floor scanning everyone I pass but she has gone, I decide to check the toilets, I pull my phone out of my bag as I walk and dial her number but her phone goes straight to voicemail. When I finally find the girls bathroom it's empty, I check all the stalls and call her name anyway but nothing. I lean back on the wall trying her phone again, still voicemail.

"Fuck!" I say behind gritted teeth. I walk to the door but Jay blocks my exit with his arm, his smile is menacing and I know I am in the fucking shit now.

"Well, well, well, look who it is. I really didn't think I would see you of all people here tonight!" His voice is low and almost quiet but it sends fear through me, like it always does. He walks towards me, I walk back, and I soon hit the wall. He traps me in by placing both his hands beside my head on the wall. "Look at you, your nothing but a cheap whore!" His gaze roams over my body and I feel sick. "I didn't bring you here because you're an embarrassment, and yet your ugly arse followed me anyway!"

"I didn't follow you; I didn't think you would be here." I say my voice small but hard.

"Yeah ok, your nothing but a desperate slag, a worthless piece of shit that isn't worth my time. I've had enough of you and your bullshit."

"Let me go then, I'll leave and never look back!" I snap my eyes narrowing to slits at him. Jay laughs in my face,

"Stupid Bitch!" He slams his forehead into my nose and I hear my nose crack, I feel the blood gush out and I fight off the black spots covering my vision, he punches me for good measure and then holds a cloth over my nose and mouth, I can smell sweets as I try and fail to take a breath, panicking I claw his arms but my movements start to feel strange. Soon the ability to even stand is hard and confusion clouds my head, what is happening to me? Jay hauls me over his shoulder and I fade in and out of unconsciousness, I try and focus but sounds are muffled and my vision is blurry. My eyes shut and I can't open them again, I feel the cold London air hit my skin before I am jostled about roughly, the sound of a car door shutting is the last thing I hear before I pass out completely.

Chapter Three

"Ugh." I groan as I come to, my head is pounding! How much did I even drink? Keeping my eyes firmly shut so the sunlight doesn't hurt my head even more I swipe a hand down my face, I hiss in pain and the memories of last night come flooding back. I sit up and my eyes snap open, the sunlight streaming in burns my eyes but I am too focused on reliving last night in my head. I remember Jay attacking me in the ladies, then being so out of it that I have no idea what happened next but I do know that this is not my home, or any home of Jay's rachet friends, so where the fuck am I? I look around the room, searching for a clue of who's house I am in but nothing, no one either me or Jay know would even know where to buy a four-poster bed like this, or have such good décor taste! I get out of bed on shaky legs and I have to stay still for a minute to stop the dizzy spell. I slowly go to the window and peek out at the beautiful garden that is huge, I have no idea where the property line stops. The rose bed directly under my window is filled with all different colours and I must say I have never seen a sea blue rose before but it is magnificent. I turn and look at the room once more taking in the details, the white fluffy rug that covers the majority of the dark wooden floor, the bedside tables which are mirrored and they match the desk and cabinet. There are three doors in the room and I head for the one closest to me, I gasp when I open it, a fully stocked walk-in wardrobe, filled to the brim with designer clothes, bags and shoes all with the tags still on them. I close the door reluctantly, last thing I need is to start obsessing about the stuff in there! I go to the next door and behind it is an end-suite bathroom, complete with a large shower, roll top bath, toilet, sink and a huge worktop that spans a whole wall with storage underneath, a stool and a mirror! I shake my head as I shut the door, I must still be dreaming! I go to the last door and spot my shoes sitting on the floor next to the frame, I am still in my dress and I smooth it down with my hands as I slip my feet in my shoes, I try the door but it's locked, my brows pinch together which hurts my head and my nose! I try it again jiggling hard but nothing, I bang on the door hard,

"Hello? I can't get out can someone come and unlock the door?" I shout, when no one comes to my aid I try again shouting and banging on the door, the noise and the effort makes my head throb and dizziness assaults me again. I slowly go to the bed and perch on the edge, hugging myself. I convince myself that this is part of punishment from Jay but a nagging tiny part of me knows that's not true, something bigger is happening and it's not looking good for me! I am pulled out of my close to spiralling thoughts by footsteps approaching and I hold my breath when the lock clicks, a stunning girl comes in, she is maybe a few years older than me. She's wearing a plain black dress and black flats, her hair is in a neat bun and she is void of makeup, she's carrying a tray with lots of different things on it but I am not interested in that.

"Who are you?" I ask,

"Just the staff, I have been sent to tell you that you may use any of the clothing and any products you like in the bathroom, your presence is required at dinner in an hour." I am taken back by her thick Italian accent but recover quickly, maybe this is a hotel? No, that can't be right, hotels don't come with complimentary clothes! She places the tray on the desk,

"Who has requested me? Where's Jay?" She ignores my question completely.

"Here is some water, some coffee and some pain killers. I will come to get you in one hour exactly." She exits the room and re locks the door, I stare at it for a moment in pure confusion. I am never going to guess what's happening so I best get ready and find out at dinner.

I am pacing the room waiting to be collected for dinner, I didn't know what to wear but I chose to be comfortable as I feel like shit and if I am honest the state of my face would just look ridiculous with a fancy dress like the ones in the closet. I picked black high waisted jeans, a baby pink ruffle shirt that I have tucked in and some Adidas trainers, I have shoved my long curly hair into a high ponytail. I did find some high-end makeup but my face hurts too much to be putting it on. My nose is most definitely broken if the swelling is anything to go by and I have big black and blue bruising under both eyes! time seems to go by slowly until finally the door lock clicks and opens to reveal the girl again, she looks over me and nods, I grab the jacket and follow her out of the bedroom door and through a gigantic house.

"What is this place?" I whisper, the girl looks at me and looks away again but doesn't answer me, I let out a little huff as I follow her down the fancy staircase, through a foyer, dining room and out a set of French doors. My eyes go wide as I take in the sunset that's a background to the expansive lawn and gardens beyond the patio where a dining table has been placed and set as if royalty were dining tonight, the large candles are lit setting a mood I am not entirely sure about. If Jay has set this up then what the fuck? He beats me, he doesn't sit me down to dinner with a sunset and candlelight! And if it's not Jay then who the fuck is it? Why am I even here and do I need to fucking panic right now? The girl pulls out a chair on one end of the table and gestures for me to take a seat and I do; she leaves back into the door we just came through. I have to take my jacket off as it's stifling here, this is not the weather we have normally in London mid-October. I am in a different country! How? I don't even have a passport! I rub my temples, something is not right with any of this, why am I so god damn calm?

"I am about to sit down for dinner, make it quick!" I hear a male's voice in the distance, I look straight ahead, squinting my eyes to find the voice but I don't see anything, until a man rounds the corner of the house and comes towards the dining table where I am sat. My mouth drops when I see a familiar face.

"What the fuck?" I whisper to myself. I manage to compose myself slightly and look blank when his eyes dart to me.

"Just deal with it! Give me an update in two hours." He shoves the mobile he was just talking on in his pocket before undoing his suit jacket and taking a seat at the other end of the table. He stares into my eyes making a shiver go through my spine, he doesn't look like the nice guy I had a cigarette with at the club anymore, he looks fucking pissed off! "Skye, who did that to your face?" He asks through gritted teeth. I screw my face up in confusion and then hiss when it hurts, Christ I need to stop doing that!

"How do you know my name? Why am I here? What the actual fuck is happening right now?" I say my agitation coming through in my voice. He leans forward in his chair and narrows his eyes at me.

"Who. Did. That?" He asks pointing to my nose,

"Jay, my boyfriend." I shrug as if it's no big deal, but I have never told anyone what he's done to me so why now and why did I just tell him? His fist balls on the table.

"Where am I?" I ask portraying more confidence than I feel.

"Italy. Forte Dei Marmi, to be precise." I try to work out how that's even possible and I go to ask but some people bring out dinner setting a plate with a dome in front of both of us, they lift the domes in unison. A fancy looking pasta dish is on the plate and my mouth waters, I am starving. The staff leave and I don't wait to tuck in, we both eat in silence but I can feel his stare on me. When I am done, I push my plate away slightly and look back up at the guy who is pushing pasta around his plate while he stares at me, I clear my throat.

"Who are you?" I ask in a small voice.

"My name is Tripada, but you can call me Trip." I nod,

"Should I be scared of you?"

"Do you feel scared?" I shake my head,

"No, but I feel like I should be." Trip pushes back his chair and I hear it scrape against the patio, he throws a napkin on his plate and walk towards me, he perches on the edge of the table next to me and I have to look right up to see his face.

"And you would be right, you are not here for good reasons Skye, if you do as your told you will be safe."

"What does that mean?"

"You can't leave, you can't run from me, at least for now, If you follow the rules, I will not hurt you or let anyone else hurt you." He runs his finger along my cheek and I feel myself leaning into his touch, what the fuck Skye this guy is keeping you hostage.

"Did you kidnap me?" I ask,

"Something like that." Trip looks me in the eyes and I see a slither of guilt there.

"Why?"

"Need to know, when your ready I will tell you. I am not a nice guy Skye so don't test me." He warns but I get the feeling that he is being nice right now, If I were anyone else I don't think he would treat them like this, with the nice room, fancy sit down dinner and calm demeanour,

"How long am I to be your hostage?" He flinches at the word,

"Until it's safe."

"I want to go home!" I say quietly but my anger can be heard.

"Well, you can't, now don't be a brat, finish your drink and then go back to your room." His face has turned hard and cold. I ball my fists at my side as I stand the chair falling back as I do. I look into his eyes,

"You can't just keep me here; you don't own me!"

"You have no idea, do you? I can do anything I want and right now, I want to keep you! Whether that's in your nice room that's fully stocked with the nice things or in the dungeon chained to the ceiling that's up to you! I mean I can beat you, is that what you like? Did you let him do that to you?" I Fume and raise my hand to slap him but he catches my hand, he stands straight pulling me to him, my body is flush with his, my wrist in his bruising grip. Trip leans down bringing his lips to my ear, "No, I didn't think so, I told you, you deserve better and I meant it!" He kisses my cheek and lets my wrist go but his hand snakes around my waist.

"You didn't mean about him, you meant about this?" I ask,
"Yeah, well I meant it for both!"

Chapter Four

"Skye." A soft voice filters through my sleep and I slowly come back to consciousness. "Skye, you have to wake up now." I put a pillow over my head and groan at his voice, I hear him chuckle and the sound rumbles through my body. "Skye, it's mid-morning and we have to go out." I lift the pillow from my face keeping my eyes shut.

"Hostages don't go out trip! You're not very good at this, let me sleep!" I place the pillow back and Trip chuckles again.

"Hostages are supposed to be meek little things shivering in the corner not telling their gate keeper they're bad at it and demanding more sleep." This time I let out a little chuckle. Trip lifts the pillow from my face and throws it on the floor and I open my eyes, I am instantly looking into his green ones.

"I have a quick stop but then we can do anything you want to do." I sit up and rest against the headboard.

"Fine but we need to have a conversation first, right here, right now!" I cross my arms to show him how serious I am. Trip Nods and passes me a steaming mug of coffee from the bedside table. I take it and hold it in my hands.

"Ok, what's on your mind?" I narrow my eyes at him,

"Really!" I say sarcastically and his lip curves at the edge. "I have no idea what's going on, the shit I do know should make me the meek, scared girl shivering in the corner but I must be wired wrong because for whatever reason I feel perfectly safe here, with you, and that in itself is fucked up!"

"Agreed." He says with a small smile.

"But I am here, I have no way of getting back to London and what's waiting for me there is probably much worse than what's here!"

"Your ex? Why didn't you just leave? Run away?" I shrug,

"I think that's why I feel ok being here, I have tried before but I ended up in hospital with a broken leg and head trauma. As much as I don't want to be a kidnappee it's better than being a punching bag!" Trip tucks a few strands of my hair and runs his knuckles down my cheek so gently it tickles.

"I won't hurt you; I promise. I am a bad man Skye don't get me wrong but I don't want to hurt you. The thing is I have taken you away from one bad guy and now you're stuck with a monster!" He pulls his hand back dropping it to his lap,

"I will make you a deal." Trip raises an eyebrow in amusement. "Two months, I stay here like a good little captive for two months then you take me back to London." Trip shakes his head.

"Six months."

"Three, and you tell me every detail of why I am here, you said last night I am not ready, well I disagree."

"Four and I will tell you in two." I narrow my eyes but I nod.

"Four months," I hold out my hand and he shakes it.

"Now can we get on with our day?" He asks and I shake my head,

"Ground rules! One, do not make me do stuff I don't want to, two, I am going to need stuff, like girls' stuff, three, if you or anyone else hurts me the deal is off and you take me home that day." Trip smiles,

"When we are out together, you will act like my date and not make a scene. You will not go around shouting kidnap, even though not one person would bat an eye and if you try to run the four months start all over, I will abide by your rules if you abide by mine, I will provide you with everything you want and need."

"Deal." I say with a sharp nod, I have no idea why but I am not going to look at my situation as a situation, I am going to treat this like a holiday and as soon as I am done sunning it up here, I am getting a therapist.

"Well, this may well be a very entertaining arrangement for both of us!" Trip smiles and I find myself returning it with a smile of my own. "Now can you get ready so we can leave?"

"What about my face, there's makeup but it will hurt to put it on."

"I'll grab you some numbing cream, and some pain killers, but you don't have to put it on, I can deal with you looking like you're a lightweight champion." I snort a laugh at him,

"I'll take the numbing cream, thanks."

I TAKE A SEAT UNDER the shade of a tree in the outside seating area of a very fancy café. Trip goes into the shop to grab us both an iced latte. I grab the sunscreen from my bag and put a big blob in my hands, I start rubbing it over my arms, legs and the bit of stomach I am showing in the crop top I am wearing. Trip places our drinks on the table and watches me as I try and reach my back and shoulder blades.

"Want some help." I sigh but nod and he take the sunscreen as I stand and turn, I grab my hair and pull it over my shoulder, His large hand rubs the cream into my skin and the feel of him touching me sends heat coiling in my core and I have to internally slap myself.

"Thanks." I say as he finishes and I turn around, he doesn't move back just stares down at me with a weird look in his eye.

"You're welcome." I take a step back and retake my seat, using a napkin to remove the excess cream from my hands. Trip shakes his head and sits down too. I take him in as he looks at his phone, he is dressed more casually today, Dark blue jeans, trainers and a tight fitted black T-shirt. His arm muscles bulge and stretch the short sleeves of his top, his top clings to his chest and abs and I can see a slight definition of his muscles that hide underneath. Trip looks younger today and his shades make him look like the cocky bad boy, he looks up and catches me staring and he smiles causing them god damned dimples to appear making me swoon.

"So, what do you want to do after this?" We have already stopped for his meeting, which was him getting out of the car looking into the boot of a car nodding and then getting back into our car. Shady as fuck of you ask me,

"I don't mind."

"Well, what do you like to do?" He asks and my eyebrows furrow.

"I erm, I don't really know."

"I don't understand, what do you do in your spare time, for fun?"

"You saw my face, right? Do you really think I was allowed to do anything I liked?" His knuckles go white around his phone and I shrug.

"Ok, then we will find out what you like to do, as we are here, we can start with shopping, every girl likes shopping, or so I've heard.

"But I don't need anything, you've already shopped for me." I smile teasingly.

"Get more, money is not an issue, you can also get some beauty treatments done, hair and stuff, then we can go home and come up with ideas of what you might like." I chuckle.

"That has got to be the sweetest offer anyone has ever made me." Trip's face lights up with a grin.

"Good, now finish your drink, you are going to have fun and I am going to groan for the next few hours." I chuckle again but I finish my drink and place my hand in his when he holds it out for me to take. I know it's messed up but butterflies are in my belly and I think I might actually like this guy, something for my future therapist, I am sure.

Chapter Five

Trip leads me into the living room when we get back to his estate, now I've actually seen it from the outside I can safely say this house is more like a palace, it's like something out of a fairy-tale. I drop down into the large white sofa and Trip follows suit once he has put the bags by the door.

"Thanks for today it was really nice." I say quietly,

"You're welcome, I had fun too." He smiles when he looks at me. We spent most of the morning shopping and then Trip sat in a salon waiting area while I got my hair cut and my nails done. "We have a few hours before dinner, what do you want to do?" He asks and I shrug,

"What do you want to do?" I ask,

"Movie?" I nod my head in agreement and he grabs the remote from the coffee table.

"OH, that one." I say as he scrolls on to Bad Boys for life. Trip presses play and gets up heading for the door.

"Popcorn?" He asks,

"Yes please." He leaves the room and I kick my heels off and get comfortable. Trip comes back with the popcorn moments later and sits right next to me, he offers the big bowl of popcorn and I take a handful. After half an hour of me chuckling at the film I move positions and I wince when I do my hand flying to my ribs. Trip notices and pauses the film.

"Are you ok?" I smile and nod but it's forced.

"Just more bruising." I shrug, Trip's jaw tightens,

"Stand up and let me see." He orders his voice hard; I should be scared of him is what I repeat inside my head as I do what he asked, I stand in front of him and he scoots forward, his legs spread so they are either side of me. His finger softly goes to the slither of skin I am showing on my waist and moves it upwards, lifting my top. He growls when he sees the bruising on my sides, his hands hover over the multicoloured skin and I feel my face going red, not out of embarrassment but out of shame. The thing is I know I shouldn't be ashamed I didn't do this; I didn't ask for any of this but yet I feel it and Trip is the only person to know I was being abused, he is the only person to see my bruises, and I have no idea why I am even showing him, maybe it's because of my face, he already knows so it's easier.

"Turn around." He snaps and I do, my back is worse covered in bruises, big bruises and I can tell how mad he is when he grips my wrist. "Why did you let him do this?" He whispers and I snatch my arm away,

"I didn't fucking let him, Trip." I snap, "I didn't ask for years of being beaten!"

"I didn't..." He turns me around to face him, he's standing now but leaning down so our faces are pretty much level. "I didn't mean it like that Skye, but why didn't you tell someone, call the police, anything?"

"Same reason I haven't with you." His eyes search mine and then he nods getting what I mean. "He took everything from me, my friends, my family, my choices, my money. I wasn't allowed to get a driving licence; I wasn't allowed to pick any job

I wanted, I wasn't allowed to do anything except from what he wanted me to do and even then, I would do it wrong! You get trapped and there's no way out, you just grin and bear it until he finally loses it and you end up in a coffin." Trip pulls me into a hug, his arms go around me and my cheek is against his chest. My arms go around him on instinct and I get this warm fuzzy sort of feeling go through me.

"I won't ever let him hurt you again, you can hate me, you can scream and shout, I deserve it, your right I am no better than him but I won't let anyone do anything like that to you again." A tear rolls down my cheek, not from sadness or self-pity but from relief, I feel relieved here like I am carefree and safe, I cling to that even though it's probably not true and the other shoe will drop any day now but I cling on to it anyway. Trip manoeuvres us so we are back on the sofa, this time I am tucked into his side. "Do you think they are broken? Your ribs I mean?" He adds when I look at him confused.

"I don't think so, if they are it's an old break."

"I will get a doctor to come and have a look tomorrow, we will get you properly healed." I nod not wanting to argue with him.

AFTER THE MOVIE AND dinner on the patio I head back to my room with my shopping bags, Trip said he had some work to do this evening anyway. I unpack the three outfits and put them in the wardrobe, take the few books out and put them on the desk. I come to the last two bags which are big ones and look around in confusion,

"Well how am I meant to use this?" I ask myself as I search the room for a TV, I mentioned to Trip that when I was a kid, I used to spend lots of time playing on the PlayStation 2 when it was raining outside and he more or less dragged me to the closest game shop and bought a PlayStation Five, all the accessories and all of the games that are out which wasn't many as it has only been out a few months. The guy at the counter explained that PS4 games can be bought on the online store on the console so he added a load of money cards to be spent on it. I decide to shower, get some comfy clothes on and take it downstairs to play.

I spend half an hour looking for a way to get the HDMI cable into the back of the tv but I can't get my hand far enough back as it's connected to the wall. I put the cable down on the table next to the console and head out of the room, Trip will know how to do it. I search downstairs in every room that has an unlocked door but there's no sign of him or anyone else for that matter. I go out the French doors onto the patio and walk along the back of the house, maybe he's out here. I soon hear quiet muffled voices and when I round the corner, I can see some torch lights flickering in the distance. I walk towards the lights and I can hear more and more as I get closer,

"Boss, he's a rat!" A man says,

"Then we will deal with him like we would any other vermin." That's Trip's voice but it's not the same as when he talks to me. I keep moving forward and stop when I see what's happening. Trip and two men are surrounding a guy who's on his knee's hands tied behind his back, the other men are holding guns to the guy's head and I can hear his muffled protests even through his gag.

"Who have you been working for?" Trip's voice is menacing as he leans down and rips the gag from the guy's mouth.

"No one, I haven't spoken to anyone." The guy is close to tears and I haven't missed all of them bar Trip have thick Italian accents.

"You know how this works right? I can make it a bullet to the brain or slice you open inch by painstaking inch, and I can always go after Mira once you're gone." I see Trip grin and it's evil.

"No, please god no!" The man cries in panic, "Proteggila, Verranno dopp di lei!" The guy has gone into full Italian now and I don't understand a word of it but he sounds desperate, Trip nods. "I Russi, I Valdikov, ti stanno cercando e non si fermeranno davanti a niente." Trip nods again once and gets his own gun from the back of his jeans, he places it at the front of the man's head just right above his nose. The bang makes me jump a little but I watch as a trickle of blood leaves the new hole in the guy's forehead and he falls to the ground with a thump.

"Oh, Shit!" I exclaim drawing the gazes of Trip and the other two guys.

Chapter Six

"Fuck!" Trip states as him and his men look in my direction. "Deal with him, I'll deal with her." He says, he sounds angry and I take a step back when he steps towards me, his gun is still in his hand and my gaze flits between that and the hard look on his face. "Let's go back to the house." He says to me and I shake my head.

"Can you put that away?" I ask pointing to his gun; he tucks it back into the waistband of his jeans never taking his gaze away from mine.

"Skye, I am not going to hurt you, I didn't want you to see that." His tone is something I would expect to hear if he were talking to a toddler.

"Trip, you just shot a guy in your garden, and you want me to go in an enclosed space with you?" I say with a shake of my head. He takes a few strides towards me and even though I am stepping back he catches me quickly.

"Are you scared of me?" He asks as he puts my arms around his waist, he places my right hand on the handle of the gun before his arms wrap around me.

"No." I whisper honestly.

"Do you trust me?" He asks and I lean back to see his eyes.

"I shouldn't."

"But you do anyway?" I nod, I know I am fucked up maybe it's a trend I really need to evaluate my taste in men. He leans down and his lips brush mine in a chaste kiss, Electricity skims across my lips, any thoughts of this being bad dissipate and I bite my bottom lip. "What are you doing out here?" He asks,

"I needed help with the TV but obviously you were busy."

"Well, I am not now." He releases me and takes my hand intertwining our fingers as he leads me back to the house.

"Trip, what was that?" I ask before we get to the door.

"I told you; I am a monster. But that was work," He clarifies and I nod and just accept his answer. I accept that he just fucking shot someone and I am not even bothered by it, and again I realise how badly I need a fucking therapist! We walk into the living room and he sees all the wires and console on the table and chuckles to himself. "Why did you not set this up in your room?" He asks and I shrug,

"There's no TV."

"Oh, well I'll get you one!"

"No, it's fine, I'd rather be in here anyway." I give him a small smile which he returns with a squeeze of my hand.

"So, what did you need help with?"

"I can't get to the HDMI ports at the back of the TV."

"Oh, I'll have to lift it of the bracket and you plug it in then I'll put it back." I nod, it's at least sixty inches and is probably heavy so I grab the wire and get ready to do this quick. Trip takes his Jacket off and throws it on the back of the sofa then goes to the TV. He grabs both ends and I watch his muscles roll as he lifts it up and off the bracket. Trip turns so the back faces me and I make quick work of slotting the HDMI into an empty slot, Trip puts the TV back on the bracket like a pro. "Do you need help to set it up?" He asks and I shake my head,

"Nah, I think I have it from here, thank you."

"Ok, I'll be in my office down the hall if you need me." Trip grabs his jacket and exits the room. I finish setting the PlayStation up.

I have just finished making an account and finally put the disk to Call of Duty: Cold war in when Trip walks back into the room with his laptop.

"Do you mind if I do some work in here?"

"Wont it be a bitch to get blood of that sofa?" I tease and he shakes his head.

"Paperwork tonight." He gives me a wink as he sits next to me on the sofa. "How you getting on?" He jerks his head in the direction of the TV.

"It took ages to set up an account and stuff but good, I am going to play Zombies!" Trip smiles and I turn to the TV; I go to the zombie menu and wait for other players to join.

"You have internet?" Trip raises his eyebrow and I nod,

"I used the ethernet cable and plugged it into the router, see. I mean have you ever kidnapped anyone before, tip, don't give hostages internet access." I point to the WIFI box in the corner. Trip shakes his head with a slight smile.

"No talking to people you actually know, and no mention of the whole you're here against your will thing." He states,

"Yeah, yeah, I know!" The game starts and I need reviving a few times in the beginning as I get used to the buttons but soon, I am shooting zombies and running around, opening doors and turning the power on.

"Kaboom!" I say as I run into a Nuke, it sets all the zombies on fire, Trip chuckles beside me. "What?" I say to him and he looks at me, I am focused on the game but I can see him out of the corner of my eye.

"Your weird, you know that right!" I shrug and he chuckles again. I soon start getting tired so I press the Netflix button on the TV remote and shove on Once upon a time, I've always wanted to watch it but I was never able to. I curl up on the end of the sofa, I soon fall asleep and the last thing I remember is Trip carrying me up to bed.

THE BETTER MONSTER

THE LAST WEEK HAS GONE by uneventfully, I have mainly played PlayStation and watched films and movies I have never been able to watch before, I have felt so relaxed it's unbelievable considering my situation! Trip always eats dinner with me and sometimes sits in the living room next to me while he taps away on his laptop, I don't know what he does but I don't think it's anything cosher! I have mixed feelings about him, when I am near him I go all teenage fangirl and can't think straight but when he's not there I remind myself he can't be the good guy, he is no knight in shining armour, but he hasn't hurt me and yes, he did kidnap me which is wrong and yes, I can't leave which is also wrong but is he that bad? Well yeah, probably but is he that bad too me, no I don't think he is. Would I have ran away with him that night at the club if he asked? I think I would have; I immediately had all the feels for Trip in the smoking area, and now I have convinced myself that I am actually right where I want to be, was I born fucked up or did I learn it somewhere? I am sat on the stool by the kitchen island sipping on my cup of coffee when Trip strolls in looking hot as hell in his tailored suit.

"Good morning, Skye." He says with a smile as he goes to the machine to make his own coffee. He comes and sits down on the stool next to mine with his coffee,

"Good morning, Trip." I reply,

"I have a luncheon I have to attend today; do you want to come?" I snap my gaze to his and a small smile spreads on my face,

"Sure."

"I will warn you though most of the guests are old men who are sticks in the mud and glamorous wives who gossip and cheat on the old men. It can be fun to watch."

"Ok, what's this luncheon for?"

"It's guised as a charity event, but really, it's just local politicians and business owners getting together to scope out the competition and to lord their successes over each other." I tilt my head a little,

"So why are you going?"

"Because I have many businesses two of which are the biggest in Italy."

"Huh, and I was starting to think you were some Mafia boss." His eyes shine with amusement,

"Who says I am not." My eyes go wide,

"Really?"

"Really, now we can discuss the different jobs I have tonight, if you want to come, you need to go get ready, it's fancy but not ball gown fancy." I slide off the stool, and start walking towards the door, I stop halfway there and spin around to face Trip.

"Wait, if you are a big bad Mafia boss by night and a business owner by day then why the hell would you kidnap me? Surely girls throw themselves at you, why the hell do you have a little London girl caged in your big house?" Trip stands and walks towards me only stopping when he is an inch from my face.

"I didn't kidnap you, I saved you, it doesn't seem like it I know but I didn't kidnap you. Trust me for a little while longer and I will tell you everything." I stare into his eyes; I have a raised eyebrow and he knows I want to know more. "I was going to be the monster everyone expects me to be, but when I spoke to you in the club, I knew I couldn't. I have this overwhelming need to make you smile and I know that's crazy because well..." Trip waves his hand around as in to say look at the situation. "I just... I don't know, I want you to see the real me, not the cold-blooded monster everyone else sees." He shrugs and I wrap my arms around his waist.

"The crazy part is I do believe you, I like it here, and I don't think you're a monster." Trip pulls away from me slightly and his hand comes up to cup my face, he leans down and his lips connect with mine in a sweet kiss. When he leans back, he is looking in my eyes and I feel like he is looking into the depths of my soul. "I best get ready." I say quietly as I back away from him. Trip straightens and nods, I turn and hurry out of the room.

Chapter Seven

The Luncheon is much fancier than I expected but I look the part with my curls straightened, a cream knee length dress and red bottom heels. My arm is looped through Trip's as he walks around the room greeting various people, most of the men comment on how they have never seen him with a woman before and the women basically dribble over him ignoring me completely. Trip leads me to a table and I lean into whisper in his ear.

"I see what you mean about the wives now, they look like rabid animals when they see you." I grin teasingly as I lean back and Trip shrugs with a cheeky grin of his own. The wait staff soon come along filling glasses with champagne and serving starters, once everyone is seated an older looking man with a beer belly gets up tapping his glass with his knife.

"Thank you all for coming, we are all here because we care about the community and our city and country and that's why this year, we are raising money for the Libera. Associazioni, nomi e contro le Mafie." I look to Trip who smirks and leans in,

"A charity that fights back against the Mafia." I hold back a laugh and try to cough to cover it.

"You're joking." Trip shakes his head. "Why are you here then?"

"Everyone in this room knows exactly who I am and what I do, and yet they all want to be my best friend. They don't care about the charity but it makes it look like they do, so the general public won't suspect any wrong doings by all the shady people in this room." I nod not understanding fully but accepting his answer.

"...so have a good afternoon and make sure you dig deep!" The man finishes as I tune back into his speech. The room is filled with light clapping and then chatter as everyone resumes talking and eating. Trip gets pulled into a conversation with the man sat next to him and I tune out of their conversation. I try the soup in front of me but it's disgusting, I push it away, I never liked fish and I can't Imagine why you would put it in soup, but I suppose this is rich people food! The rest of the Luncheon goes by quickly, we eat the main meal and desert, Trip has lots of people approach him and they all talk to him like, as he said, they want to be his best friend. We duck out early as it's boring as hell talking to the stuffy old men.

"So, what did you think?" Trip says as we slide into the back of his goon driven SUV.

"Eh," I shrug and he chuckles,

"Boring I know, but I have to make an appearance every now and again."

"So, what now?" I ask as the car pulls into the traffic.

"Well, I have the rest of the afternoon free, how about we go do something fun!"

"Like what?"

"Bowling." I chuckle,

"Really? You want to go bowling?" I hold back the chuckle that I am holding.

"Why not." I shrug and then nod my head. "Take us to a bowling alley." Trip says to the guy driving.

"OMG, you suck!" I say laughing when Trip's ball ends up in the next lane. He lifts his arm and rubs the back of his neck,

"I thought this game was meant to be easy, throw the ball knock down pins!"

"Maybe try and roll the ball, not launch it!" I exclaim, I get up and grab my ball, I don't do no fancy footwork or anything just put some power into rolling the ball down the middle. "Strike!" I turn and give Trip a grin. Trip walks past me to grab his ball and he playfully bumps his shoulder against mine, I laugh when he runs towards the lane and his ball bounces down it when he lets go.

"Fuck! This is hard!" He grumbles.

"Do you want to quit and play at the arcade instead?" I suggest and Trip pouts and nods like a toddler which makes me laugh harder. "Come on tough guy." I say as I walk in the direction of the arcade games.

Arcade games are more Trip's games, he is currently smashing the record on an updated version of pacman, I watch him as he concentrates, His dark green eyes narrow on the screen, his lips pulled into a thin line and his big hands thrash about the joystick and the buttons. When he finally gets killed by a ghost, he puts his name in and he watches as he rises to number one on the leader board, he turns to me, he's grinning and he looks so handsome when he's carefree.

"And that is how it's done." He puts his arm over my shoulder as we walk away from pacman.

"I think we have played them all." I say smiling up to him.

"One left and then we can go home." He walks us over to the grabber machines and I snort a laugh,

"You are never winning this, they are rigged."

"You want to bet on that." He grins and I shake my head, He taps his game card, that's loaded with money, on the pad and uses the joy sticks to manoeuvre the grabber, when he presses the button, the grabber comes down but Trip completely missed. After waiting for the grabber to go back to its starting point, he tries again, this time he grabs the big penguin teddy and it lifts up and just as it gets towards the hole it has to be dropped into to win it falls down.

"Fucking stupid game." Trip mumbles as he tries again. He goes for the penguin again; his aim was good but the grabber didn't close enough to get it. "Wait here." He says sounding frustrated. I stand in front of the machine sipping on my milkshake as Trip goes off to do god knows what. He comes back a few minutes later with one of the staff members in tow and she opens the door, "What one do you want Skye?" I narrow my eyes at him and he looks smug as hell right now.

"The teddy bear, please." I say to the girl. I expect her to grab the normal sized one but she doesn't she grabs the big one that is hung up at the back of the game. She hands it to Trip who looks ridiculous holding a bear half the size of him but I can't carry it I have my drink.

"Thank-you." He says to the girl as she hurries away. I step closer to him and he shuffles the bear so it's not blocking him from me. I am half an inch from my body touching his,

"Did you threaten that poor girl or give her money?" I ask teasingly,

"I have no idea what you are talking about, I merely mentioned the game was broken." He winks and I chuckle.

"Thank-you." I whisper as my hand reaches up, I grab the back of his neck gently and pull his head down, I press a kiss to his lips feeling that electric dance along my own as I do. We pull away but we stare into each other's eyes for a long minute. Trip clears his throat before taking my hand and we walk out of the arcade.

Chapter Eight

A few days go by and I don't really see Trip which for some reason has put me in the worst mood, I feel extremely bored and a little needy. I've heard him in his office shouting at whoever is in there or down the phone and I have left him to it, it's not something I need to get myself involved with. I am watching Miranda when I hear a load of banging from Trip's office, I get up and walk towards it popping my head through the door as I knock.

"Are you ok?" I ask, Trip's head is in his hands and he slowly looks up to see me, he looks angry.

"Fine, what do you want Skye?" I stand frozen in the doorway,

"Erm, I just wondered if you were alright and if you wanted to take a break come watch a film with me for a bit." Trip laughs but it's not out of humour, this laugh is dark and scary.

"For fuck's sake! Skye, I am not your boyfriend, you know that right? You don't ask me for shit! If I want your attention I'll come and get it!"

"Alright, no need to be a prick!" Anger floods my system and I shake with the strength of it.

"Actually, there is, are you really so vapid! I have kidnapped you, you're a fucking hostage! Act like one and hide in your room! I don't want to fucking see you!" I just stand there, not really knowing what to do. Trip Bangs his fists on the desk as he gets up from his chair. "Don't be a fucking stupid bitch right now, Skye, just go before I make you!" He actually shouts this at me and I turn and stomp back to my room. What the actual fuck! This is the real him, isn't it? I have done it again, fell for the lies. I pace the room biting my nails, I need to get out of this house. Making my decision I rummage through the wardrobe and grab the workout clothes and trainers. I get changed and put my hair up in a ponytail, I make my way downstairs trying not to be seen by Trip and head out the french doors and on to the patio, I do some stretching and then take off, the nights breeze feels cool on my face and I pound my feet hard as I run into the huge gardens. I let a few tears fall from my eyes as I run. I can't believe I was so stupid, what is wrong with me will I never learn? I hear shouting behind me and turn my head to see a few men are chasing me their guns out. Shit! I don't even know if these are Trip's guys or not. I run harder turning slightly so I am running back towards the house, the men are gaining on my fast and I push myself to run as fast as I can. I can see the side door of the house and I push myself to get there before I am gunned down but I don't get any further one of the guys jumps on me sending me crashing to the ground. When he gets off of me and I turn over I have five men surrounding me all with guns pointed at my head.

I lift my head when the large metal door opens and Trip walks in looking even more furious than before, I have been down in this dimly lit room for what must have been a few hours, my arms are tingling as they are cuffed to chains connected to the ceiling, it's painful because my arms are stretched so far above my head and I have been on tip toes the hole time to ease that a little. Trip comes and stands in front of me and I force my face to be blank.

"Why did you run?" Trip asks quietly,

"What!" I ask, does he think I was running away?

"I told you not to fucking run!" I flinch as his words boom around the room, "You think I want to see you like this, I fucking told you the rules!"

"Fuck you Trip!" I snarl, he comes closer to me and grabs my chin with his hands and his grip hurts me, I don't make a sound but tears of pain roll down my cheeks, he sees them and loosens me a little.

"You said you wouldn't run from me!" He says as he stares into my eyes,

"You said you wouldn't hurt me!" He Immediately steps away from me and runs his hands over his face. He turns and walks towards the door.

"Are you fucking serious! You're just going to leave me chained up in here?" I scream at him and he stops in his tracks when he turns, I see the guilt in his eyes.

"I warned you of what would happen." He turns away from me but doesn't leave.

"You know what! Fine, leave me here, at least now I see the real you! No longer will you pull the wool over my eyes and make me fall into some sick sense of false security." Trip's hands ball into his fist by his side before he leaves, then the door is shut and I hear the locks click.

Tears are streaming down my face when the door opens slamming against the wall, I glance up and see it's Trip and look away, I can't wipe the tears from my face and I can't stop them either. It's only been about half an hour since he left, why is he back? Is he going to kill me now? I flinch when he rushes towards me, he reaches up and unlocks the shackle on my wrist, my arm is completely dead now so it just falls on his shoulder and I don't have enough strength to move it, he unlocks the other one and my legs buckle under me, Trip catches me easily and lifts me so he is carrying me. I sob into his chest as he walks out of the room with me in his arms,

"I am so fucking sorry Skye." He says as we go up the dark staircase, this makes me cry harder. I hate that he is seeing me like this but I can't stop it, my emotions have finally surfaced and the force of them all has opened a god damn river of tears. Once we are in my bedroom, I expect him to let me go but he doesn't, he climbs on the bed and I am on his lap still crying into his chest, it takes a while but the feeling starts coming back to my limbs and the painful pins and needles help the with the crying, letting my anger manifest and start to take over. I push away from him and scramble off the bed, it takes a lot of effort and I struggle standing upright but I do it.

"Leave!" I snap, Trip gets off the bed but stays on the other side.

"Please Skye, let me explain."

"There's nothing to explain! I want you to leave!"

"There is, Skye please, just hear me out?"

"I don't want to hear anything from you, just leave me alone, you can lock me in here for all I care just fucking leave!" I am shaking with pure fury while I shout at him, Trip lowers his head and makes his way towards the door.

"I am sorry." He says quietly before leaving shutting the door behind him. I let out a sigh before shaking it off and going for a shower, my body aches all over and the hot water beating down on my skin is uncomfortable, I wash and dry quickly and throw on a tank top and some sweats and get into bed, it's still dark outside as it's around two am. I don't sleep even though I need too, I lay there awake for hours. I hear the door open quietly and feel the bed dip on the other side to where I am laying now pretending to be asleep, I really want to tell him to leave but I can't be bothered to argue with him right now. I know it's Trip instantly, I get this feeling when he's near, like something is pulling me too him from the inside.

"I know you're going to hate me when you wake up, and I wouldn't blame you, I am everything that's wrong with this world. I tried to be different with you and I failed, I thought I could save you from him and I did, but I've put you with me and I am so much fucking worse." Trip laughs quietly and it's a sad laugh, it makes my heart hurt more than it already does. "I actually convinced myself we could have something, be something. How fucked in the head is that! Thinking you, the kind, sweet, funny, smart, beautiful girl would ever give her kidnapper a chance, that you could ever see me as something other than the guy keeping you locked up in a big house!" Trip leans over and his fingers trace my skin as he pushes my hair off my face, without thinking my hand goes to his wrist when he pulls it back, I open my eyes and they lock on to his in the dark. There are so many emotions in his eyes that they look stormy.

"I don't hate you." I whisper, "I should but I don't, I didn't try to run away, I was upset because you treated me like shit and went for a run, I tried to get back to the house, back to you when I was being chased by men with guns."

"I know, it didn't sit right with me, I didn't want to believe you would run from me and I watched the CCTV, your outfit, stretching and your trajectory told me everything I needed to know. I am so sorry you got put down there, I am sorry I left you down there! I am fucking sorry I hurt you. I should never have said those things to you, I didn't mean any of it." I sit up and scoot closer to him on the bed, I wrap my arms around his neck and hug him hard, his arms wrap around me instantly and he burrows his head in my neck.

"I forgive you, Trip. As fucked up as you are, I am the same, I think we could have something too. I feel stuff I can't explain when your around me. Since I've been here, I have felt kind of happy and that's because of you." Trip lifts his head and his hands cup my face making me look into his eyes, he looks between them, looking for deceit maybe? He leans his head closer to mine and our lips are almost touching. He wants me to bridge the gap, he is giving me the choice. I close the space and kiss him, it's soft at first but passion wins out and it deepens, his tongue skates along my bottom lip and I open my mouth for him. Our tongues clash together and my hands end up in his hair, there's no electricity on my lips with this kiss, no light tingling, instead it's sparks, sparks that start on my lips and travel up and down my whole body, Trip pulls away suddenly and rests his forehead on mine. We sit there silently looking into each other's eyes before Trip clears his throat.

"You need to sleep." Trip moves to get off the bed but before I even think about it the word leaves my mouth.

"Stay." Trip pauses, his back to me, but then he kicks off his shoes and I watch him as he takes his shirt off his back muscles rolling as he does, heat pools in my belly as I watch him strip down to his boxers, my eyes roaming every line of his incredibly fit body. He gets into bed and pulls me down so I am half on him, he pulls my leg over his and his hand rests on my thigh, his other hand curves around my back and his finger draws little circles on my hip, my head is on his hard chest but I've never felt more comfortable and my own arm goes around his waist. No more words are spoken and I thought I wouldn't be able to sleep but the next thing I know is that I am waking up in an empty bed.

Chapter Nine

"Morning." Trip says as he gives me a peck on the lips. He has his young carefree look today making me smile.

"It's the afternoon!" I say back and he shrugs going to the coffee machine and making me a coffee.

"Do you want to take a trip with me?" He asks, a little nervously as he puts the drink in front of me, leaning over the counter on his elbows.

"What kind of trip?" I ask raising an eyebrow,

"No work just me and you, in Milan."

"Milan, really?" Trip nods, his half grin distracting me completely, how is it even possible to look that good. Like does he have genes passed down from gods?

"Ok." I smile and his grin gets wider,

"Go pack a bag, if we leave in an hour we can get in the hotel and get settled in time to go to dinner." I slide off the stool and grab my coffee. "Skye, you don't have too, you can just stay here, I don't want you to think you have to do anything with me."

"I know, I want to." I smile and his smile returns, I turn and leave the room, excitement building. Milan, I am going to Milan!

Trip is waiting for me in the hallway, I didn't know what to pack so I kind of packed one of everything just in case, Trip takes the large bag from me and throws it over his shoulder, he takes my hand and intertwines his fingers in mine. We start walking down the stairs and I look at him with a raised eyebrow,

"What?" He asks when he notices me looking at him,

"Did you not pack a bag?"

"Yeah, but mines already in the car."

"Oh." I reply, we head out of the main door and a sleek, silver, two-seater car is sitting there.

"You're driving?" I ask as he walks me around to the passenger side and opens the door for me.

"Yeah, like I said, just me and you." He shuts the door and opens the boot to put my bag in before getting in the driver's side. Trip presses a button and the engine roars to life; he presses another button and the roof goes down. I hurry to put my hair in a bun with the hair tie I had on my wrist, I will never get the knots out if I leave it down and with my hair, I can't brush it if I am not in the shower with a ton of conditioner in it.

"Ready?" Trip asks in a chuckle and I narrow my eyes at him.

"Ready." I reply, with my response Trip puts his foot on the accelerator and the car speed up quickly down his long driveway. We turn out of the property and on to a country road and even though we are going very fast, I find myself relaxed. Trip handles the car with ease and he winks at me when he catches me looking at him. After a while of staring at the gorgeous landscapes I turn to Trip,

"Can we put some music on?"

"Yeah, grab my phone and choose what you want." I reach to the middle of the windshield and grab the phone from the stand and go to Spotify, I choose the chart hits playlist and it comes through the car's speakers. I put the phone back in its stand and start singing along to Sweet Melody by Little Mix. The rest of the three-hour drive goes by quickly, I sing along to most of the songs that play and Trip chuckles as he watches me out of the corner of his eye.

We pull up to a grand hotel, I step out of the car when my door is opened and stare at the big stone pillars.

"Welcome to the Excelsior Hotel Gallia, please follow me to check in." A man in a suit greets us and we follow him as other staff get our bags and a valet parks the car. This place is amazing, it looks old from the outside but the inside is modern and screams luxury!

"Hello, do you have a reservation?" The girl behind the reception desk asks,

"Yes, Tripada Berluscioni." Trip answers and she taps her fingers on the keys of her computer.

"Ahh, Mr. Berluscioni, we have been expecting you, the Katara suite is ready for you, please let us know if you need anything." She hands Trip a key card and we go the lift; Trip presses the bottom for the top floor. When we enter the room I gasp, this place is gorgeous.

"Go, look around." I do as I am told, the living area has four white sofas surrounding a glass coffee table which reflects the chandelier above it, it has these golden lamps too, I've never seen anything like them. I continue through the different rooms and find four bedrooms all huge in size with grand beds, one even has a curved wall around the head of the bed. There's a dining room with a sleek black table and ten chairs with a huge vase of white orchids in the centre. There's a bathroom with his and hers sinks and a sauna, a dark room lit up with calm blue lights with a jacuzzi built into the floor, a second smaller living room, and not one but two outside areas, and they are not small either, fully furnished with sofas and tables. I take a seat outside and just look out at the incredible view.

"So, do you like it?" I turn my head at Trip who is leaning over the back of the sofa slightly.

"Like it! It's amazing! But do we really need all of this?" I ask feeling a bit guilty, this must have cost an absolute fortune.

"No, we don't need it but I like it, it's the best hotel room in the world, and you have to stay in the best at least once." His response makes me smile. An older man knocks on the door that leads out to the terrace, he's wearing a suit and has a white cloth over his arm.

"Sir, Madam, I am your personal butler for today, the concierge has put your bags in the master bedroom, is there anything else you need?"

"Could you please book us a table at Seta for around two hours' time? An outside table if possible?" Trip asks and the butler smiles as he nods and retreats.

"ARE YOU SURE WE ARE not overdressed." I ask looking down at the blood red gown I have on. It is sleek and fits me with perfection, it's floor length and the thick straps cross over at my back which is fully on show. Trip gets up from the sofa and walks towards me,

"No, and even if we were no one could deny that you are the most beautiful woman they have ever seen in that dress." I blush and dip my head, Trip's hand comes up my arm and round to the back of my neck making my skin tingle where he touched, my hair is in a fancy chignon giving him complete access to where his hand is. I look back up at him and his gorgeous green eyes glitter, he leans down and kisses me sweetly. When he pulls back, I bite my lip and his eyes widen at the sight. "Come on." He says as he intertwines his fingers with mine. Once we are outside Trip turns to me, "Are you ok to walk, it's only around the corner." I nod and he leads me down the street. I take in the sights around me, Milan Really is beautiful and I have only seen one or two streets. We turn the corner and it takes us a few more steps before we are walking into a beautiful restaurant. The waiter leads us through the inside and to our seat in the garden, our table is small and intimate and there are two candles in the middle of the table. Trip pulls my chair out for me before he takes his own seat. The waiter brings a bottle of Dom Perignon over without us even asking and pops the cork, pouring some into each of our glasses before putting the bottle in the ice bucket standing next to our table.

"Trip, thank you for bringing me here." I say almost too quietly, Trip reaches for my hand across the table and gives it a squeeze.

"I am sorry, Skye and this isn't just me apologising, this is me treating you how I wanted to all along. I want to see if we can have something together, I don't know how that can ever work now but I want to try."

"Ok, I can do that." I say and the smile that spreads across his face lets me know this is the right decision, I know that I am this close to falling for him despite everything, and that is either very fucking stupid and I should rush finding a therapist or it could be the best choice I will ever make. I can't help but feel like there is a hell of a lot I don't know about this situation I find myself in and not just because he told me so either, I cannot find it in myself to make him the villain. I know he's not the villain in my life, I don't know how I know that but I do, I can just feel it.

The meal is amazing as expected and I am a little tipsy when we leave, Trip takes us the long way back to the hotel and we stroll through the streets hand in hand, we don't talk just enjoy each other's company, I am a bit disappointed when we arrive back at the hotel but I push that aside. When we are in the lift, Trip turns to look at me,

"I had an amazing night." He has a small smile and I return it,

"So did I." We stare into each other's eyes and the tension builds between us. I step into him and pull his head down and I kiss him needily, he returns my kiss with the same intensity. This dress is the only thing stopping me from climbing him like a tree. The lift dings as the door opens and we break apart both panting, Trip takes my hand a fire in his eyes and rushes me into our suite. When the door shuts, he slams my back into it before pressing into me with his body and restarting the kiss the lift interrupted. My hands grip his jacket pulling him even harder into me before I reach up and slide it off his shoulders. I then start unbuttoning his shirt and my hands roam over his hard muscles when they're exposed to me. His hands roam across my body making my skin feel like it's on fire. He pulls back and looks me in the eyes, I can see the hunger there and I am sure mine look exactly the same.

"Are you sure about this, we can take it slow." If anything, that sentence right there just makes me want him even more.

"I am sure." I reply and with that he rips my dress, it falls to the ground, and I am left in black lace lingerie and blood red heels.

"Fuck!" He whispers before his mouth finds mine again. He picks me up and my legs wrap around him, my arms holding on to his shoulders, he doesn't stop the kiss as he walks me to the bedroom. He puts me back on my feet when we are at the foot of the bed and his hand traces down my neck, over my collarbone and over my breast, I slide his shirt off of him and unbuckle his belt. He kicks his shoes, socks, and trousers off before he picks me back up and sits me on the bed. He lifts my leg one at a time and takes my heels off, throwing them across the room, he trails kisses up my leg and across my body until he reaches my mouth again. His hands roam my body and stop when he gets to my breast, he pulls down the cup and his fingers find my nipple, I moan when he rolls it between his finger and thumb. He smiles against my lips before he dips his head down and puts my nipple in his mouth his hand going to my other one, my back arches as heat pools between my legs. His mouth goes to my other breast and his hand roams downwards very slowly, his fingers trace my skin and I ache in anticipation, he finally slips his hand into my underwear and he slides his fingers into my folds, I moan again and his head lifts up.

"Fuck, Skye, your so wet." He murmurs, His fingers circle my clit and I am close to coming already, he moves his hand down and he puts a finger inside me curling it and I bite my lip.

He adds a second finger and they start to move as his thumb circles my clit, his fingers pump in and out as he pushes me closer and closer to my orgasm, he kisses my neck and all the way down to my nipple, when he tugs gently on the hard bud with his teeth my orgasm hits hard making my legs shake, he doesn't stop though and when I've come down a little, he pushes my panties down my legs and throws them towards where my shoes went, he stands at the foot of the bed in-between my legs and pushes his boxers down. I stare at his hard length with wide eyes, that is going to hurt. He moves to his bag and I scoot up the bed and take my bra off, He produces a condom and rips it open with his teeth as he comes back to me, after he has rolled it on, he climbs on the bed and in-between my legs. He stares into my eyes for a moment and I nod, knowing the question he is silently asking. He positions himself and I lift my knees for him. He slowly puts his tip in me and I moan, he slowly enters all the way in and there is a bite of pain before I am adjusted to him.

"Shit, Skye." He says as he drops his head to kiss me, he goes from leaning on his hands to leaning on his elbows over me and he starts to move. I moan into his mouth and he starts to get faster and a little harder, he lifts my leg a little higher and he hits the spot only a few men can ever find and it blows my fucking mind. My back arches making it feel even better and I soon am burying my face into his neck as I climax again, he slows while I ride out the aftershocks and then he flips us so I am on top of him, my hands rest on his chest as I move, he's even deeper in me now, how that's even possible I don't know. Trip's hands find my face and he pull me down to kiss him and I oblige happily, his hands go to my hips and they grip me tight as he helps me with my movements, I cry out when another orgasm hits me, harder this time and I see stars! He follows me over the edge quickly thrusting into me twice before letting go.

"Fuck! Skye!" He moans, I roll myself off of him and I tuck myself into his side, I am so relaxed and sated I nearly fall asleep, Trip gets up and I watch as his naked self goes to the bathroom, I bite my lip, Trip comes back with a wet flannel and spreads my legs, he cleans me up which I have to ignore how awkward that makes me and then after disposing of said flannel he gets back into bed and tucks me into him.

"I think we could do that every minute of every day and I still would want you even more." Trip whispers into the quiet room. I lean up and kiss him,

"Is that a challenge?" I tease and Trip groans.

"Go to sleep, Skye, we have a long day tomorrow." I don't even ask what we are going to do as I yawn and get comfy laying my head on his chest as he runs his fingers down my back.

Chapter Ten

I wake up before Trip and after mentally telling myself it's creepy to watch him sleep I get out of bed, I throw on his shirt from yesterday and find my underwear from my bag, I head out of the bedroom and call the butler with the phone by the door.

"Butler service, how may I help."

"Hello, can I get some coffee and some breakfast please."

"Certainly, we have a great chef's special breakfast would you like me to order that?"

"Please, Two servings if possible."

"Certainly miss, it won't be long." I wonder around the living room taking everything in and it's not long before there's a quiet knock at the door, I open it and the butler comes through with a tray, he places the coffee on the dining room table and exits. I pour my cup and take a sip, god damn this is good coffee! I sit there deep in thought when Trip walks into the room wearing nothing but grey sweats, I can see every line of his body including the irresistible v lines. He kisses me before he takes his seat next to me.

"Good morning gorgeous." He smiles at me,

"Good morning." I smile back, his eyes run from my messy hair down to his shirt and to my bare legs.

"You don't know…" A knock at the door stops him from finishing his sentence. He gets up and answers the door, when he comes back, he's pushing a little metal trolley that's probably got our breakfast in it. Trip parks it near the table before coming back to me and holding out his hand, I take it without question and he kisses me. "The only breakfast I want is right in front of me." Trip pushes a chair away from the table and he picks me up, kissing me again, he places me on the edge of the cold glass and his hands roam, he goes straight for my underwear and rips them off. He runs kisses down my neck and then kneels on the floor his tongue darting out and licking my clit. I moan as my head drops back and my hand goes in his hair. His tongue laps at my clit, he varies his pressure and then he nips me, his fingers dig into my thighs stopping me from moving.

"Ahh, fuck!" I moan as he slides two fingers into me and starts pumping them. He doesn't increase his speed and its wonderful torture, "Please Trip." I pant and he lifts his head,

"Please, what?" He grins but I am not ashamed to admit I am desperate enough not to care,

"Fuck me, Trip please just fuck me." Within a split second he's up and I have been taken off the table and bent over it. The cold glass on my nipples sends me even crazier. Trip pulls his sweats down a little and I hear him rip open a condom packet. Moments later he thrusts into me hard and I scream out, he thrusts hard and fast as his hands grip my hips.

"Fucking hell, Skye, you're so responsive." I feel my pussy tighten around him as an orgasm gets closer and closer. I clamp around him as I scream out, Trip grunts as he comes a moment later and he collapses on my back, he soon puts his bodyweight on his hands and we both catch our breath, I moan a little when he pulls out of me. He turns me around so he can kiss me and it's an intense kiss. Trip pulls back and cups my face with his hand. "Best fucking morning." He states before walking off I assume to the bathroom; I find one of the other bathrooms and we both get back to the dining room at the same time. Trip serves the breakfast and I pour him a coffee and we sit next to each other as we eat, his hand on my thigh the whole time.

"So, what are we doing today?" I ask,

"Some sightseeing and then we have to get on a flight, I'll explain on the plane."

"Ok." I reply.

"So, hurry up with your breakfast then we can get ready and go," I nod taking another bite of some amazing, scrambled eggs and slide my chair back.

"Go get us a table, I am just popping over there quickly, if the waitress comes ill have an iced latte and a muffin." Trip says as we enter the outdoor seating area of a little café, Trip goes across the street and disappears into a shop. I think about all we have seen this morning; the best part has got to have been seeing da Vinci's last supper. This whole trip has been perfect and I can't stop myself from smiling, I never thought I would ever see another country, let alone be in Milan and with a guy that makes me feel the way Trip does. It almost feels too good to be true, but I can't let myself second guess this, not with him.

Trip comes back just as the waitress brings out our drinks and his muffin.

"What time is our flight?" I ask,

"About an hour, so once we have finished here, we need to get going." I nod and sip on my drink. Trip's phone rings and he gives me an apologetic look as he answers,

"Yes." Trip answers, "You have got to be joking, she just quit! Two weeks before the company launches! Where the hell am, I going to get a PR manager in the next twenty-four hours to handle the launch." I know someone who's great at PR; shame I can't bring her here. But why can't I she doesn't have to know the ins and outs; I could tell her I ran away and Trip helped me do it! Hope builds in my chest at the thought of seeing Millie. "Find me someone and do it quickly." Trip hangs up the phone and he looks pissed.

"You're probably going to say no but, my best friend would be a great PR manager, and I kind of need her, I could tell her some story instead of... well you know." Trip looks at me and it's a pitying look,

"Can we discuss this on the flight?" He asks and I nod giving him a small smile, I knew it was a long shot anyway.

When we get back to the hotel our car is already parked out front and our bags are being loaded into the boot, Trip tips the staff and opens my door for me. It's a ten-minute drive to the airstrip where a jet is waiting on the tarmac. I turn to Trip as he stops the car,

"How can I fly; I don't have a passport?" I ask and Trip studies my face for a moment.

"Actually, you do. That's another thing we need to discuss on the flight. Come on, I'll tell you everything once we are in the air."

I sit nervously in the plush seat of the jet opposite Trip as I wait for the hostess to do her checks, get us some drinks and go through emergency procedures, he's going to tell me everything, like why I am with him? It's bad isn't it, whatever it is it's going to be fucking bad. My leg starts bouncing through nervousness and I avoid looking at Trip.

"This is your Pilot, please wear your seatbelts as we take off, I will inform you when your free to go about the cabin." He says,

"Thank you, we won't need you for the rest of the flight, feel free to have a drink and relax." Trip says to the hostess and she grins at him. Soon we are alone and the plane has taken off, I finally lock my gaze onto Trip's and he points to the brandy that's on the table in front of me,

"You might want to drink that first." I lean over and grab the drink, I down it and the fucker burns, Trip covers his laugh as I screw my face up.

"Ok, go." I say, Trip clears his throat.

"I told you before that I didn't kidnap you, and that's almost true. Your ex, he sold you."

"What?" I say my eyebrows furrowing,

"He sold you to the Mexican cartel, the one that deals with sex slavery in particular." I stare at him, like what the fuck! How do people even sell people?

"So how do you have me?" I ask,

"The Mexicans owed me a favour, a big one. They asked me to grab you for them, I agreed but when I saw you working in your shop months ago, looking sad and broken, I knew I couldn't give you to them. Long story short they no longer owe me anything."

"Wait, months ago?" Trip nods,

"I was meant to take you months ago, that's why I had a passport for you, but I couldn't do it, I followed you for ages every spare day I had I went to London to see you, the Mexicans stalled your ex, when I saw you in the club that night, I had to speak to you, and when I did, I knew I couldn't let you go. I made the call, it's my fault he hurt you in that bathroom."

"It's not your fault, he would have done that or something else to me, regardless." I say and I know it's one hundred percent true.

"There's more, you asked about your friend, that's not possible."

"Why not?"

"Jay faked your death, we are going to your funeral now." Trip looks at his hands and I just stare at him.

"You said I could go back to London." He snaps his head up to look me in the eyes,

"And I meant that, I didn't know he would do this, I did some digging, the night I thought you ran, that's why I was so angry, he took out life insurance on you and he got the payout. I was angry because I can't let you go back until it's safe and now, he might have ruined that for you."

"How much did he sell me for?" I don't know why but this is Important to me,

"Sixty thousand."

"That's It? That's how much my life was worth?" A tear escapes my eye and I quickly swipe it away, Trip undoes his seatbelt and comes to me, he undoes mine and sits me on his lap putting the lap belt back over the both of us.

"No, no amount of money will ever compare to what your worth." Trip places a kiss on my shoulder, "I am so sorry Skye, if you want to get out, I can set you up anywhere in the world, just tell me and I'll make sure your safe, but you can't be seen in London." I nod understanding what he's telling me.

"Millie, she won't tell, we can take her with us." I am practically pleading and the squeeze Trip gives me lets me know that it can't ever happen. I take in a deep breath and let it out composing myself.

"Ok, I can never go back." I say cementing that fact in my mind. "So why are we going to my funeral?"

"I just thought you should see it for yourself, see what he did for his own gain." I nod.

"Let's go and get out of there as quickly as possible, I just want to go home." I say.

"Home?"

"Yeah, where we live." I look at Trip and he hides his smile.

"Never thought I'd hear you say that." I roll my eyes at him and I move so I can rest my cheek on his shoulder.

"Thank you, Trip." I whisper,

"What for?"

"You saved me from two evils, Jay and whatever horror show waited for me in Mexico."

"Don't thank me, I would do it again in a heartbeat."

Chapter Eleven

We get to the Funeral first and we hide on the disused balcony on the second floor which can look down to the service. Trip had a change of clothes for us on the plane and we both are now dressed appropriately for the occasion, I even have a wig on, a platinum blonde, sleek straight wig, cut into a fashionable bob. Trip said it suited me but it's so different, add in the black shades and I know I won't be recognised if I am even seen. My funeral is as pathetic as my life has been, four people at my funeral not even enough people to carry my coffin! Jay looks like his dickish self him and his mate don't realise that a black adidas tracksuit is not proper attire for a funeral. My dad is here and he looks sad, but the kind of sad you get when your hamster dies not your daughter. Mum is nowhere to be seen the fucking bitch, and then there's Millie who is sobbing into a tissue as she walks beside my coffin and places her hand on it. The priest or whoever stand up and goes to the podium,

"We are here to lay Skye Brackwell to rest, her life which was so short was ripped from us, and we all will mourn her with all of our hearts." Then he goes right back to his chair and stands there.

"Is that it?" I throw my hands in the air as I whisper to myself.

"I am sorry, Skye." Trip says and I turn to him,

"Stop apologising, none of this is on you." I look back to my shit service and everyone is leaving already, everyone except Millie who is sitting at the front and watching as my coffin goes into the back where they will set it on fire. I hear her let out a cry and I tense up, almost going to stand, I let the tears fall as I silently say goodbye to the only fucking person, I had in this world no matter what. My best friend and my only family. I see Trip looking between me and her and I feel him tense.

"Go, we will sort it, go get your friend." He lets out a breath and I wrap him in a hug.

"Thank-you!"

"I'll go lock the doors then you can come down." I watch him as he leaves, what the hell am I going to say to her, it's not every day you turn up to your own funeral! Trip is back in minutes and I practically run down the stairs, when I get down there Millie is standing in the middle of the aisle, like she can't make herself leave. I creep up behind her,

"I fucking love you." She gasps and spins around, her eyes go wide and I pull off the shades, Millie smiles and pulls me into a hug.

"How? What?" She pulls back and puts her hands on her hips. "Explain!" She tells me off.

"I can give you the long story later but in a nutshell, Jay sold me to be a sex slave, Trip..." I point up to him, "Saved me and took me to his home in Italy, I thought I had been kidnapped until about two hours ago, Jay faked my death to claim life insurance and I think I am falling in love with my now not kidnapper." I shrug and Millie's mouth falls open.

"So why are you here?"

"Trip thought I should see for myself, also you can't tell anyone about me being alive, especially not Jay."

"Yeah, of course." She pulls me into another hug.

"You can come with us you know, leave this shithole and come to Italy."

"What now?" She pulls back but doesn't let me go, I nod. She doesn't even think about it, "Let's go." My grin matches her and Trip is already waiting at the side door for us.

"We need to go." Trip says as he opens the door and makes sure it's clear for us to leave and get to the car.

"Just get what you need, I can get you whatever you want, I can also get your stuff packed up later and have it shipped over, grab your passport." Millie nods as she exits the car and runs across the road to her flat. I climb on Trip's lap, straddling him and I crush my lips on his. I pull back and stare into his eyes,

"Thank you, you don't know how much this means to me."

"This is what will make you happy, of course I'll give you it, and I am falling in love with you too Skye." I feel my face heat and I put my lips on his pouring everything into it, when we pull apart, we are both panting and Trip smiles. "I'll do anything for you." I nod and climb off his lap and look out the window, minutes feel like hours while we wait for Millie but she's fast, she runs back to the car with a rucksack in her hand.

"Ready?" Trip asks her and she nods, Trip puts his foot down and we speed back to the airstrip where the jet waits for us.

MILLIE WHISTLES AS she enters Trip's house for the first time and I chuckle,

"Millie I'll get the staff to sort your room out just give me half hour."

"Thanks." Trip shows her the living room where she has no issue getting comfy and putting on Netflix, Trip takes my hand and leads me up the stairs. I thought we were going to my room but we turn in the opposite direction and stop outside a door. I look at Trip and he looks almost nervous.

"I, erm, well I asked the staff to put your stuff in here while we were gone, if you want to go back to your room that's ok, I can have everything put back."

"Okay..." I reply, Trip opens the door and leads me in the room, I look around for a minute and realise this is his room. The walls are a light grey and the furniture is a black glass, the bedding is black and the room is kind of bare. It has everything in but nothing that says this is someone's bedroom.

"You don't like it, it was stupid, I can get your stuff moved back." I spin and face him,

"I do like it, I was just thinking there's no bits and bobs, like photos and stuff." Trip smiles,

"That's because I filled the rest of the house with my shit, it's so spread around no one even notices." I laugh and he pulls me into him, his hand running through my hair. "So, you don't mind being stuck in here with me every night?" I shake my head.

"Are you sure you want to be stuck with me in here every night?" I ask, Trip leans down and kisses me sweetly.

"I can't think of anything I want more!" I blush again and my stomach fills with butterflies.

"Good, you can give Millie my room, it's already set up."

"Yes ma'am." Trip kisses me on the forehead before he leaves the room and I look around, there's a door either side of the room, one to the huge walk-in wardrobe where all of Trip's clothes are on one side and mine have been put on the other. The other door leads to the en-suite, and it's double the size of my old one, with his and hers sinks, a big countertop and a shower that can fit an army in. Never mind the bath sat in the middle of the room. My shampoo and conditioner are sat in the rack next to Trip's shower gel and my makeup has been put in the drawers. Looks like I am all in, I smile at the thought, the old me is dead, the Skye that had no life, who was battered every day has been buried and now I can start my life again with Millie here and Trip I couldn't want anything more.

Chapter Twelve

"So, I was thinking we should go out for dinner, make Millie's first here special." Trip shrugs and I love the idea,

"Make the booking, how long have we got to get ready?"

"An hour and a half."

"Ok, I'll go tell her." I grab the soda off the kitchen counter and head up to my old room, I knock on the door before poking my head in.

"Hey, Girl." She says and I shut the door behind me and sit on her bed, she's busy putting the few bits she had in rucksack away.

"We need to get ready, we are going out for dinner, and if I know Trip it will be a fancy place." I wiggle my eyebrows at her.

"I have nothing to wear!"

"You can borrow my stuff; I have lots of stuff now." I roll my eyes,

"Look at you, being treated like a princess." Millie's smiles and I blush.

"Listen, I know you explained everything to me on the plane, but we need to talk just me and you." She raises her eyebrows,

"I know, you must think I am stupid being with him…" Millie cuts me off,

"Not about Trip, he's good for you, I can see that! About Jay and how you never fucking told me, I could have helped you." I shrug,

"What to set him on you, no thanks."

"You said you took pictures; I want to see them." Millie demands,

"Not tonight, can we just go out and have fun, I will see if I can get Trip to get them from the cloud tomorrow." Millie's face softens and she pulls me into a hug.

"Don't ever hide anything like that from me again! I will run anywhere with you; we are family and we don't let family suffer alone." I nod and we both well up, no tears fall but both of our eyes go glassy with moisture.

"Ok, let's get me a dress!" I lead Millie out of her room and down the hall to mine and Trip's bedroom, I poke my head in and Trip is buttoning his shirt,

"Millie needs to choose a dress." I tell him and he smiles, He grabs his jacket and his phone and comes to the door pushing it open,

"It's all yours." He kisses me cheek before heading towards the stairs, "I'll be in my office, if you need me." He shouts back to us as we enter the bedroom.

"Ok, Clothes and shoes, that door. Makeup and hair, that door." I say pointing to each door in turn. Mille goes straight for the Wardrobe and starts scouring through everything.

"Why does most of these clothes still have tags on?" She sounds pissed and I laugh.

"Seriously? I haven't really had the opportunity to wear all of that!"

"Ok, this one for you!" She throws a midnight blue jumpsuit at me. "These shoes..." She hands me the shoes. She goes in a drawer I didn't even know was there and she gasps, I go over and look into the drawer too.

"I didn't even know these were here." I say looking at the sparkling jewellery, there's necklaces bracelets, earring and watches.

"Ok, this, this and this." She hands me a few bits and I roll my eyes at her; I place my outfit on the bed and go back to watch her choose her own. Millie goes for a black dress with lace inserts at her waist and her thighs, she chooses a pair of silver stilettoes to go with it.

"No jewellery?" I ask,

"No, that's yours, I can borrow your shoes but not that." I smile at her,

"That's stupid!" We both head into the bathroom and I show her where everything is, we both had showers after I put her in her room so we don't need to worry about that.

"Sit, I am thinking dark Smokey eyes with a light glitter on the inner corner, bold lipstick and sleek straight hair."

"For you, you mean?" Of course, she shakes her head.

"You're lucky that I am so glad you're here right now, do what you must." I wave my hands and let her dress me up. It's always been her go to, she loves treating me like her own personal barbie, but I can't lie, even though I am not used to the makeup and the clothes, I do love when she pampers me like this.

By the time we are both done Trip is waiting for us in the kitchen, When I walk in his eyes go wide and then they darken, his gaze travels from my feet in the glittery strappy shoes that are way too high, up my legs where the jumpsuit has slits on each side from my ankle to the top of my thigh, up my bare arms and finally at my face.

"Well tell her how pretty she looks then." I smile at Millie telling Trip off, he clears his throat.

"You look amazing." His voice is husky and I bite my lip smiling. He looks to Millie for a split second and back to me, "You both do."

Millie rounds the counter and opens the fridge, grabbing a bottle of wine and placing it on the counter, she soon finds three glasses and pours the wine. Trip comes to stand behind me his arms around my waist and his chin resting on his shoulder.

"She made herself at home fast." He whispers and I chuckle.

"Just so you know, you're the third wheel tonight, not me."

"The boys are going to love her." Trip chuckles in my ear and I turn in his arms,

"What boys?" I narrow my eyes at him.

"So, I kind of kicked out my best friends while you have been here, they are coming back tomorrow."

"Well, that was rude, and ok, I don't need to worry about them, right?" I ask,

"Nah, they can just be a little playful." His gaze goes from me to Millie and back to me. Right, they are all going to love Millie.

"Oh, and Rina is coming back too, don't worry she's like my mother, she is Luca and Tiao's Mom, and she looks after us, she's excited to meet you." I nod my head; this big empty house is going to get a whole lot smaller.

"So, are you American or Italian." Millie continues her interrogation of Trip and I sit at the table slowly eating my chicken salad enjoying the show.

"Italian but I was sent to an American boarding school, I stayed there from the age of seven to nineteen, then came back to take over the family businesses when my dad stepped down."

"And what is it you do for business, like your legit ones, I mean?" We told Millie about the Mafia thing on the plane; it wouldn't have made sense why he ended up with me.

"I have a few, but they are all owned by me under A.D.A industries. I do have a job opportunity for you though, Skye said you were in PR?"

"Yeah?" Millie looks dubious and I hold back a chuckle,

"So, I have a new line of hotels launching in two weeks and the PR manager just quit, she said it's too much for her she couldn't handle the job. If you think you're up for it, I will gladly hand that job to you."

"Oh, I can handle it." Millie grins,

"Ok, do a good job and I'll keep you on at A.D.A industries. Ill sort out a contract tomorrow."

"What about me, can I have a job? I Imagine I am going to be very bored while everyone else is working." I pout and Trip chuckles.

"We can find you something, I am sure; I have something for you though." I push my plate aside as he produces three boxes. He gives one to me and one to Millie. "I want you both to know that my home is your home now and you are free to leave whenever you want," I open the box and inside is a credit card with my name on it and a set of keys, I look over to Millie and she has the same.

"We don't want your money Trip." I say,

"I know but If you girls need anything or want to go out shopping or whatever, it's there, the boys have the same, no spending limit, money is not an issue, you both are family now and what's mine is yours. And the keys well, Skye I didn't do this right at the beginning, you are safe to go do whatever you want, just not in England, all I ask is that if you do leave, you take me, one of the boys or one of my guards with you, that goes for you too Millie, my people will drive you around all day every day, they are there to keep you safe so use them." We both nod in unison, and I feel all emotional. I am officially not a hostage anymore and yet I wouldn't leave for anything. "Ok, now that's dealt with, here." Trip passes me the other box and I untie the bow, inside is a beautiful charm bracelet with two charms on it. One is the Italian flag and the second is of the Duomo di Milano, the cathedral we visited in Milan.

"Thank you, Trip this is beautiful." He takes the bracelet from me and grabs my hand pulling it closer to him, he clasps the bracelet around my wrist and kisses my hand before letting it go.

"Aww, look at you two." Millie states grinning. I swat her arm and she laughs. "Are there any clubs around here?"

"There are, but there is no way I am going clubbing with you two on my own, we can go out drinking tomorrow." Trip says and Millie pouts.

"Fine, but tomorrow night best be the best night ever!"

I AM WOKEN UP TO LOTS of shouting from downstairs, I burrow myself deeper into Trip's side, groaning.

"I think the boys are back."

"Mmmm " I reply, pulling a pillow over my head, I hear Trip's muffled chuckle. He wiggles around and moves himself, so his nose is touching mine under the pillow.

"Time to get up, babe."

"I need more sleep!" I groan,

"Really, what if I did this?" He presses his lips to mine and I have to fight myself, so I don't kiss him back. "No. What about this?" His lips trail kisses down my neck and over my chest, I am still naked from last night and probably have smudged makeup all over my face. His tongue flicks my nipple and I stop the moan that threatened to come out. I feel him smile against my skin as he licks and kisses his way down my body until he is between my legs as soon as he licks the sensitive nub I moan. He teases me with his tongue and finally he pushes a finger inside me making my back arch, his movements are slow and lazy, drawing out every ounce of pleasure from me. I come quickly but the orgasm lasts an eternity once I have recovered, he gets off the bed and heads for the shower.

"Are you fucking kidding me?" I grumble, Trip winks at me before he disappears from the room completely. I throw the covers off me and follow him into the bathroom, he is already in the shower the water gliding over his skin. I go to the counter and wipe off my makeup with some cotton pads and makeup remover, I was right I looked like a racoon. By the time I have finished brushing my teeth he is out of the shower and his scent washes over me, Trip smells amazing, he has this cedar smell with hints of cinnamon and lavender. I tie my hair into a bun at the top of my head not wanting to wash it today, it takes forever to get straight so I like to keep it that way for a couple of days. Trip leans into me from behind and kisses my shoulder, he moves his kisses up to the part of my neck that drives me insane, I turn in his arms and kiss him hard. It doesn't take him long to give in, he picks me up and places me on the counter, he digs through a drawer and finds a condom, he makes quick work of rolling it on and coming back to me, I place one hand on his shoulder and then he pushes into me hard, I cry out when he is fully inside me, he fucks me hard and fast and he is moaning right along with me. My head falls back and I lean on the hand that's on the counter, matching his thrusts with my hips, his hand roams down my body igniting a line of fire on my skin.

"Fucking hell, baby." I come hard and I feel my pussy clamp around him, making him come too, his head comes to my shoulder and my arms wrap around him as we both come down from the high.

Once I am dressed and I have some light makeup on I head downstairs, Trip left me to shower and he went down to go see everyone. I am handed a coffee by Trip as soon as I walk into the kitchen, I smile nervously when four sets of eyes land on me. Three guys get up and come towards me,

"I am Luca, Trip's second in command." The older blonde guy nods,

"I am Tiao, Luca's much hotter little bro." Tiao comes to me and puts his arm around my shoulder. Trip playfully slaps him around the head, Tiao pouts and goes back to his brother.

"And I am Paul." The brown-haired guy says holding his hand out, I shake it.

"We picked him up from America, he never left." Tiao Teases. They all are just as built as Trip and Luca and Paul are just as tall, Tiao is a little bit shorter than the others, when they are together there is no doubt, they are fucking intimidating.

"Shoo, shoo, you will scare the poor girl." The older woman swats the guys out the way and she pulls me into a tight hug. "I am Rina, Luca and Tiao's mother. You don't know how happy I am to meet you." She says in her thick Italian accent, she pulls back not letting me go and turning to Trip. "Assolutamente sbalorditivo, sei felice?"

"Molto felice." Trip smiles as he replies to her, Rina gives me another hug before letting me go and going back to her drink on the counter. Everyone goes back to their seats and I take the empty one in-between Trip and Rina.

"Millie not up yet?"

"Millie huh? How many girlfriends did you get while we were away?" Trip narrows his eyes at Tiao who looks pleased with himself,

"Just the one, Bro, Millie is Skye's best friend and she lives here with us now." Luca and Tiao look at each other and race off the stools pulling each other back as they exit the kitchen. Paul and Trip roll their eyes in sync and I chuckle,

"Should I go and help her?" I ask Trip and he shakes his head,

"She will have to deal with those two herself." Rina hurries out of the room after them, shouting in Italian. I hear the commotion upstairs for a good ten minutes.

"Ow, no need to hit people!" That was Tiao, was that Millie or his mum, I bite my lip to hold back a laugh, Millie walks into the kitchen looking furious.

"Oh, come on, we didn't mean anything." Luca says,

"You woke me up, you crowded my personal space, you started asking me shit, then he grabbed my arse!" Millie fumes as she comes to stand by me.

"No need to punch me though." Tiao comes in next rubbing his cheek.

"I may have forgotten to mention, Italian women are tough, but British are next level." Trip adds unhelpfully.

"Thanks for the warning, dickhead!" Tiao says, both guys retake their seats and Rina hurries to get Millie a coffee.

"I am sorry about my boys; they are still pubescent." Rina narrows her eyes on her sons and I spit out the coffee that I had just sipped as I choke on a laugh.

"Mom!" Luca and Tiao say in unison.

"We have some work to do this morning, we will be in the office of you need us."

"Don't worry about the girls, I am going into town they can come with me." Trip looks at me to see if I am ok with that and I nod.

"Use your cards if there are no transactions I will be pissed." He raises his eyebrow; I roll my eyes at him and Millie draws a cross over her heart with her finger. I turn to Millie when he leaves,

"I don't feel right about spending Trip's money."

"Me either, maybe we can spend like the minimal just to stop him whining."

"Girls, if you want something get it, Trip provides for all of us because he is the head of this familia. We can have everything we want and need because of the danger we are all in by being here with him. We all do things to help him out and you will too, I cook and clean and take care of everyone, the boys work for him and he can find you both a job too, he will pay you but he would rather you spend his money, just let him do that for you, it eases his guilt."

"Guilt about what?" Millie asks,

"The bad things he has to do, being the head of a Mafia." I think out loud and Rina nods,

"Not only that but he has enemies, he will always have enemies and they have come after him and us many times s, he hates that everyone is put in danger because of him. That's why there are so many guards, he wants to protect us."

"Can't he just quit the Mafia; he has other businesses?" Millie asks, Rina shakes her head.

"If he steps down from the head of the Familia, his cousin takes over and if that happened it would be bad, Trip maintains peace in Italy, he deals with crime yes, but he controls it, he stops hundreds of thousands of innocent people getting caught in the crossfire, but Arnaldo, he wants it to go back to the old ways, where no one was safe, it was the Mafia and only the Mafia! The old ways were bad, there was no peace just wars, the Russians, the Mexicans, the Americans all wanted the Italian Mafia dead and buried. Trip has stopped most of that and has amicable relationships with them."

"So, we just spend his money how we see fit, because he feels guilty?"

"And it makes him happy, he wants to give us all everything." Millie and I nod our heads, it still doesn't feel right but I suppose it makes a little sense.

"So are we going shopping today then." It took Millie no convincing at all really, did it?

Chapter Thirteen

"Ok, I feel guilty now." I say as we enter the house, shopping was fun and it's safe to say me and Millie went overboard, Rina was a bad influence too pressurising us to buy everything we tried on in the designer shops. From Louis Vuitton to Prada to Mac to Gucci, and now we have too many bags to carry.

"Nonsense, you'll see." Rina smiles as she heads to the kitchen with the few bags she has.

"Your back! Did you have fun." Trip comes over and kisses me on the cheek, he bends down to the bags I have put on the floor.

"We did, but now we feel bad, we spent so much money!" Trip's face lights up with a huge smile. "Never feel bad about spending our money, we are all in this together and the money is there to be spent, I make how much you two spent in what? Probably less than an hour, trust me, someone has to spend it!" Millie splutters,

"We must have spent like fifteen grand, if not more." Trip nods,

"You make fifteen grand in an hour?" I ask not believing him,

"More like Fifty, you didn't spend much at all!"

"Are you sure he's not an alien and we are now living in some sort of alternative universe?" Millie asks and I chuckle,

"Ok now I don't feel so bad, we basically did a Primark shop in comparison to a normal person."

"Oh, and those came for you two earlier, Millie your contract is over there too." Millie walks over to the table and picks up her contract and two packages, she hands one to me, it has my name on it.

"What are they?" I ask,

"I ordered them for you yesterday, you both want jobs so you're going to need those." Trip starts to walk towards the stairs, "Can someone help Millie with her bags?" He shouts down the hallway, The next thing we see is Luca and Tiao fighting each other to get to her first, she shakes her head and walks past us and up the stairs leaving the two boys to fight over her bags.

"Do you need help putting all of this away?" Trip asks as he places my bags on the bed.

"No, the best part of shopping is unpacking it when you get home!" I state, Trip comes to me and kisses me sweetly,

"I love it when you call this place home."

"What else would I call it, it's the only place I have ever felt at home." Trip stares at me with an adoring look on his face, I smile before snapping him out of it. "Don't you have work to do?" I tease and Trip nods,

"I'll be done by dinner, Rina is cooking our favourite, were going to leave around Ten for the club."

"I forgot about that. I best get in the shower; Millie is going to want to dress me up again." I roll my eyes and Trip laughs.

"You could go how you are and you would be the most gorgeous girl in the room, but I must admit she makes you look like a badass!"

"Yeah, yeah, she is wonder woman with makeup!" I tease as Trip goes back to work. I sit on the edge of the bed and open the package. I roll my eyes but smile at what's in the box, an iPhone, of course the newest model, an apple watch and an iMac. I turn on the phone and it's already set up, a message comes through,

Trip: I hope you like it.

I quickly type my response,

Me: how could I not xx

We all take our seats on the patio dining table, Rina sits and lets the other staff bring out our food, Trip is at the head of the table, I am next to him Tiao is next to me Rina is next to him, opposite Rina is Paul then Millie and finally Luca who is opposite me. The boys chatter among themselves while Millie plays with her new phone and I just people watch for a minute. Once everyone has their food in front of them Rina gets up and everyone stops what they're doing to give her their full attention.

"I would just like to say how very happy I am to welcome Skye and Millie into our family, it's about time we had some girls around the house." Trip squeezes my knee under the table and I give him a smile. "La famiglia e per semre!" I look to Trip to translate but I don't need to in unison the boys raise their glasses and say,

"Family is forever!" With that everyone starts eating the best lasagne I have ever tasted, when we have all finished the meal in record time, the conversation starts up again.

"We are going to take Millie to the office tomorrow afternoon, show her around a bit." Tiao says as he winks at her,

"Actually, we are all going to the office tomorrow afternoon, any ideas on what job you want?" Trip asks me and I shrug,

"I don't know, I don't even know what I would be good at!"

"You were good at loads of things in school, do you remember those marketing ads you did for graphic design, they were awesome."

"Really, we could always use more of that!" Trip adds,

"I haven't touched a graphic design programme in what five years, I wouldn't even know where to start."

"Well, you have a laptop now, maybe give it a go, and I am sure I have an old iPad and a pen around here somewhere ill dig it out. We can trial stuff until we find what you want to do."

"Ok, it can't hurt I suppose." I shrug, but the thought of doing something has a little excitement brewing in me.

"Ok, now we need to go get ready," Millie states as she swipes two bottles of prosecco off of the table and heads towards the door, "Are you coming?" She asks me and I rush out of my seat,

"I have been summoned." I say to Trip as I go to Millie.

"THIS CLUB IS AMAZING." Millie says as we lean over the balcony to see the main dancefloor, the music is loud and proper dance hits are being mixed by a DJ and the crowd is all for it. Trip comes up behind me and puts his arms around me leaning his chin on my shoulder.

"Do you like it here?" He asks and I nod.

"Good, maybe the next one in this chain I'll name Skye." I turn my head to look at him,

"You own this place? Of course, you do." I should stop being so shocked when he reveals stuff like this, I mean we have the VIP section to ourselves and bartenders have been bringing over drinks all night.

"Come on, I am bored up here with the old men, let's go dance." Millie shouts over to me, she grabs my hand and we head down the stairs and she plants us right in the middle of the dancefloor. I look up and see Trip watching me, his eyes darken as my hips move to the music. Tiao punches him in the arm before he heads down the stairs too. I focus on Millie who is smiling at me, she leans in and shouts in my ear,

"You two are really cute."

"Shut up!" I say rolling my eyes,

"No seriously, I have never seen you so happy and full of life, it suits you." I pull her into a hug and she hugs me back with a laugh, when I pull away from her Tiao is there and he whisks her away from me, I laugh and he winks. I turn to head back to the VIP section but Trip is there, he pulls me close to him and starts moving to the upbeat music, I follow his lead. After a few songs I am hot and I am really horny, so I gesture to go and get a drink, Trip takes my hand as we walk back to our table. No one else is here, I spot Tiao and Millie grinding on the dancefloor and I laugh,

"I think Tiao has won her over." I say pointing in their direction.

"That does not surprise me. Looks Like Luca has moved on anyway," I look for him and finally I see him in a dark corner of the club making out with some rando,

"I like the guys by the way, they seem cool."

"They are good guys; I am glad you like them and they like you." I smile at him and he tucks me into his side, I lean forward and grab a cocktail from the table of never-ending drinks. Tiao and Millie soon appear and Millie looks panicked, she visibly relaxes when she sees me,

"Are you ok?" I ask when she sits next to me and pulls me in a hug.

"Sorry you disappeared and I got worried." I flinch a little knowing this has something to do with the last night out we had. I smile at her and she smiles back.

"Millie, do you have any cigarettes?" I ask, my bestie normally has my drunk smoking stash but I doubt she got some this time. She shakes her head and I pout.

"What's up babe." Trip says when he sees my sad face.

"I haven't got any cigarettes and I am dying to drunk smoke right now." Tiao laughs,

"What the fuck is drunk smoking?"

"When you smoke but mainly when you've had a few drinks, Moron!" Millie tells him and I laugh with Trip.

"Paul should have some, wait here ill grab them." Tiao says as he walks back to the dancefloor. Tiao waves us down from the balcony and gestures for us to go to him, we all get up and go down the stairs and Tiao leads us outside to where Paul is standing with a cig hanging out of his mouth. He offers me the box and I pull one out quickly, Paul holds up the lighter for me and then I am sucking in all of the smoky goodness.

"Better?" Trip asks,

"So much better." I reply making them all laugh. We all chatter while I smoke away and when I am finished, I stub it out in the ashtray and lead us all back inside, just before I get to the door a guy bashes past me,

"Ow." I say my hand going to my shoulder, he doesn't see Trip and the others and looks back to me

"Watch where you're going then, stupid bitch!" I don't even blink before Trip is gripping the guy by his throat, his veins on his hand popping out. It's hot I admit, but fuck he is angry.

"Who the fuck do you think you are, that's my girl you just insulted and hurt." Trip growls and the guy's face pales.

"Shit I am sorry; I didn't know she was yours." Paul, Tiao and Luca step around Trip and the guy,

"See the thing is, it doesn't matter whose girl she is, you fucking hurt a girl by being a dick and then didn't apologise, instead you mouthed off to her!" Tiao says his anger showing in the tick of his jaw. Trip lets him go but punches him in the face for good measure,

"Take him out, make sure security knows he has a lifelong ban." Paul and Luca escort the dickhead past me and Millie loops her arm in Tiao's.

"Are you ok?" Trip says his hand running over my shoulder,

"I am good," I nod, Trip kisses me hard and my knees buckle slightly.

"Ugh, get a room." Tiao says and we pull apart from each other,

"Why I have a club." I laugh and so does Millie, Tiao just rolls his eyes and we all follow him back inside.

Chapter Fourteen

"What you up too?" Trip asks as he enters the bedroom, I am sat on the desk with the iPad he gave me messing around on some DJ app that was on it,

"Not a lot, just messing really." I continue tapping on the screen and I can hear the music in my ear,

"You ready to go?"

"Yeah, sure." I save the track and put the iPad on the bedside table, I slip my shoes on that I left at the end of the bed and grab my bag putting my phone, purse and shades inside. I move to where Trip is watching me at the door and go on my tiptoes too kiss him, he leans down so I can reach him and the kiss is electric like always even though it is brief. Trip takes my hand and we walk downstairs to where everyone is waiting in the big foyer. Millie comes to stand next to me and she leans into my ear,

"I have a new trick. Wanna see?" She grins evilly and I nod my head a few times. "Oh, Skye I am so thirsty, I could really use a can of coke right now." She uses her most dramatic, oh woe is me voice and I raise an eyebrow at her she jerks her head towards the guys and I look at them, Luca and Tiao look at her and you can see the determination cross both of their faces, they look at one another and then glance towards the kitchen.

"Fuck no!" Tiao says as they both start running, Luca puts his foot out and Trip's Tiao so he lands on the marble floor, Tiao then grabs Luca's leg as he passes him and now, they are fighting on the floor, soon they both get up shoving each other as they race to the kitchen. I start laughing hard and Trip just shakes his head,

"Do you have to encourage them?" His voice is full of amusement and Millie just shrugs as a response. Tiao and Luca reach Millie at the exact same time, each of them holding a can for her,

"Thanks boys." She says on a laugh as she grabs both and hands one to me. "Cheers." She hits her can on mine and winks, I laugh again as Millie struts her stuff towards the door.

We pull up outside a skyscraper that looks like it's made out of pure mirrors, it was only a half hour drive which is a lot shorter than I was expecting, Trip slides out of the car first and I follow, then Paul slides out, the others are getting out of the other car in front of us. Trip puts his hand on my back as he walks us into the building. The lobby is huge and there is a full security counter checking all visitors, there is a large reception desk and seating areas dotted about. The place is full of people coming and going some are even just having a chat. We all go over to the lifts and when we get in Trip presses the number fifty-five, of course he would have the top floor. When we step out, he is greeted by a young guy maybe a little younger than me,

"Mr. Berluscioni, I have updates for you two of your accounts and I have emailed that too you, you're meeting at One has been pushed back to Three and I am still looking for a PR

Manager to take over for Gia." We all walk behind Trip and I think his assistant,

"Thank you, Matt. I have found someone for the PR position, and the contract has been signed, I will email it over to you later today."

"Brilliant, can I get you and your guests anything?" Matt asks,

"No thank you, can you check in with the Caribbean team and get an update, I feel like they are avoiding us."

"No problem, I'll get on that straight away." Matt veers off and goes to a desk that is sat outside the big office we are heading too. Trip opens the door and we all pile into his fancy office. There is a large wooden corner desk on the right side of the room behind it is a big backed leather chair that looks comfy as fuck. By the window is a large meeting table with eight chairs and it looks out too an amazing view of the city. There is a small bar in the corner on the left side, an electronic fireplace with two tv's on top, one is CCTV of the building and one is playing the news, a few bookshelves are on top of the TVs, holding folders and the odd book. We all take a seat at the table, Trip hands Millie and I a small folder each. I open it and the first page says A.D.A Industries, below there is a table of contents.

1. A.D.A Tech and Telecommunications.
2. A.D.A Hospitality.
3. A.D.A Spirits.
4. A.D.A Marketing
5. A.D.A Publications

"What is this?" I ask, looking up to the guys,

"That there is a portfolio, which has eighty percent of our businesses in it." Luca says with a grin.

"Jesus, that's a lot of stuff to own!" Millie says flicking through the pages.

"And we are always expanding." Tiao adds.

"So why are you showing us this." I ask,

"Because you want jobs, Millie is on PR for the new hotels right now but after that she will be doing PR for everything, when it is needed. And we touched on marketing for you, we have a big marketing department that we outsource too so that's an option or we can look to see what you like." Trip says.

"Ok so what floors are A.D.A's, I don't want to be ending up at work for a different company." Millie says jokingly,

"All of them." My jaw hits the table,

"All of the Fifty-five floors of this huge skyscraper?" I ask, All the guy's nod at once.

"So, what do you guys do?" Millie asks,

"We are all co-owners, and we don't have a board of directors, no shareholders no one else to answer too." Trip answers,

"But in simple terms, Trip is like the CEO, we all report to him, I am in charge of operations, Paul is in charge of finance and Luca is like the president, which is basically an assistant to Trip." Tiao winks and we both chuckle as Luca throws a pen at his head.

"So how come you have all been away for weeks, and you have been at home for weeks, wont that impact on your work here?" I ask them,

"Well, we were still coming in, Trip worked from home so it didn't Impact us much." Luca answers,

"But I do need to come in more, everything is going back to business as usual." Trip says shooting me a sympathetic smile.

"Speaking of, you have that Gala on Friday." Luca says to Trip.

"Don't remind me. Skye you are going to need a ball gown."

"Oh, don't drag her there, that's torture!" Tiao says, Me and Millie laugh.

"So, what should we do today?" I ask, knowing the guys are going to be busy.

"Take a look around, go for lunch or you can go home, it's up to you. The cars outside take either one wherever you go the driver will be your security for the day." Trip says and I nod, I look at Millie who shrugs,

"I could do with some lunch and then we can go back and read all about this massive corporation." I nod,

"Sounds like a plan." I say and we get up from the table,

"See you guys later." Millie says and we leave the office.

The day goes by quickly, we spent a good two hours looking around all the different floors and getting a feel for the place, we didn't get lunch in the end and just came home, Rina made us both a sandwich and we sat at the breakfast bar while we read through the folder. I head up to chill in our bedroom after we have finished as Millie wanted to work on her PR stuff for a bit, I showered got into some sweats and a tank top and go back on the iPad, I do some graphic design stuff on the apps I downloaded this morning and I must admit it looks really good but I don't think I could do that full time. I have no idea what I want to do, I just know I want to something, I want to work and I will take whatever Trip offers me but I should really find out what I want my goals to look like now I can actually achieve them.

Chapter Fifteen

The rest of the week has dragged, Trip and the guys have been working hard and have rarely been at home before dinner and then they are going out in the evenings to take care of some less legit businesses. Millie has been going to work with them, now she is in her role fully I have been here alone and bored. Rina has been helping me figure out what I want to do for a career but we aren't getting anywhere and it's making me feel deflated. I have spent the afternoon being pampered and polished by a team of people, my hair has been moulded into an intricate updo that I am not allowed to touch, my makeup has been done to perfection giving me a light look, my nails are now not mine and they are longer and painted a matte grey colour. I am sat in the kitchen watching Rina as she reorganises a cupboard waiting for my dress to arrive.

"Oh, I know, what about animals?" Rina asks and I snort a laugh,

"No way!" I reply and she comes to me,

"What did you want to do growing up, what did you like?"

"I never really knew what I wanted to do, I thought maybe I would figure it out when I had to choose for college but I never got that far and then Jay forbid everything and I lost all hope for any future really."

"I think that it will just hit you, like fate will take control and you will be pushed into it." Rina says with a grin,

"What like some random job will just fall in my lap and I won't even realise it's what I was destined to do?" Rina nods happily and I laugh again, "Well then, let's hope it happens soon." Someone coughing at the kitchen entrance makes me spin on my stool.

"Miss, a parcel for you." I look away from his face and to the huge box he is carrying, he places it on the counter in front of me,

"Thanks." I say as I go to open it.

"Not here, I don't want to see it until you have it on." Rina says with a motherly smile, I nod, pick up the box and run upstairs. I pull out the dress and it is next level gorgeous. It is a tuille halter neck that comes down in a plunging neckline that doesn't stop until the skirt which starts at my waist, it has no back and no sides, and the skirt comes out in proper ball gown fashion. The whole thing is black and on my upper body the only thing covered is my breasts. I quickly and carefully strip out of my comfy clothes and put it on. I look in the mirror and I feel a little overwhelmed, I have so much skin on show and I don't even feel conscious about it. I turn and look at my exposed back, it is weird to see my skin so normal. I don't think I have had zero bruises in years and it is hard to get used too. I go over to my wardrobe and pick out some shoes, I go for simple black strappy heels as no one will see them under this massive dress anyway. I grab a black clutch and pop my stuff in it before heading out the door. I hear the door open as I start walking down the staircase and I look over to see the guys and Millie, they all have stopped just inside the door and are staring at me, my brows crease together,

"What? Does it look bad?" I ask stopping in the middle of the stairs.

"Fuck no! You look amazing." Millie says snapping out it first, she elbows Trip who clears his throat. He comes to me and holds out his hand I take it as he escorts me down the rest of the stairs. I swat his hand away when he reaches up to cup my face,

"The makeup girl will kill me!" I say and he smiles.

"How do you get more beautiful every time I see you." He says quietly and I blush, he leans in and kisses me lightly, I hear a gasp from behind him and we both look round to see Rina with tears in her eyes. "Magnifica!" She whispers, she shoos Trip away from me so she can circle me before hugging me tightly. When she is done with me, she turns to Trip.

"Go get ready, quick! You will be late and it is rude to keep Skye waiting." Trip runs up the stairs taking two at a time at Rina's telling off. Millie loops her arm in mine and leads me to the kitchen, I look ridiculous sitting at the breakfast bar in this dress, the guys have disappeared and Millie is busy popping open a bottle of champagne. Millie hands me a glass and I sip on it, not wanting to be drunk before I even leave, she tells me all about her day at work and what she has been doing to Tiao and Luca.

"I thought that Tiao had won you over?" I ask,

"He did but I haven't told them that yet." I laugh at her grin and shake my head,

"You are evil!" I say laughing some more, I see a flash come from the kitchen door and turn to see Trip holding his phone and looking at the picture he just took. I look over him from feet to head admiring how he looks in a tux. The guy is hot! Like lava hot!

"You got ready fast!" I say,

"Bonus of being a guy, shower in five seconds and put some clothes on." He says with a cheeky grin, he is leaning on the door frame and it makes him look like a model. "Car's outside, shall we?" He asks, I slide off the stool and give my glass to Millie.

"See ya later, bitch!" She says as I loop my arm in Trip's.

"Let's get this over with so I can get you home and out of that dress!" Trip whispers in my ear, oh I am looking forward to that!

The car door opens and Trip gets out first his hand coming back in to help me out, I am blinded by flashes of cameras as we start to walk down the red carpet. Trip smiles at the paparazzi and I follow suit suddenly feeling really uncomfortable. When we enter the building, we are directed in front of big boards to have more pictures taken, Trip put his arm around my waist as we smile for the camera's, I try to look confident but I do not feel it at all, I never expected this. The people taking the photos are shouting Trip's name and asking him who I am, am I his girlfriend and all sorts of other questions, Trip does not respond just moves up the line stops for more photos and moves again. It takes a while but soon we are in the main room where the event is taking place. We are taken to a table near the front of the stage and we sit, champagne being handed to us.

"You could have warned me about the photo shoot." I say in his ear,

"Sorry, I didn't even think about it."

"What even is this Gala for?" I ask,

"This is the Annual Gala for Italian Entertainment achievements, so an awards ceremony for the famous."

"So why are you here?"

"Because I am finalising the deal to buy out a big production company, so a lot of the tv shows and movies nominated tonight will technically belong to me soon."

"Right, anything else you want to buy? The moon?" I tease, he just rolls his eyes at me but a smile is plastered on his face anyway. It doesn't take long for the tables to fill up, three people join us at our table and Trip introduces us, one is a beautiful blonde actress called Viola, her agent and the guy that is selling the production company. Viola sits next to me and moves her chair so she can see the stage better,

"It's so nice to meet you, Skye. What do you do, are you a model? That dress is magnifico!" She says in a rush of excitement and I chuckle,

"No, I am not a model, I haven't chosen a career path just yet, I am working on it."

"Si, Si, Camiellia, you think she has model potential, no? Get on that she will be big star, do not let her slip through your fingers." The agent nods her head quickly and starts tapping away on her phone. I look to Trip for help and he shrugs, leaning in so his lips brush my ear.

"Viola can be intense but she is not wrong, you could be a model." He pulls back and winks, now is not the time to tease, I wouldn't know how to be a model let alone my curves. I am most certainly not model material. I let out a sigh of relief when the music starts and the host is introduced on stage.

THE BETTER MONSTER

Halfway through the show my bag vibrates on the table, I pull my phone out and check it under the table.

Millie: OMG, you need to check the celebrity news in Italy, NOW!

Me: Huh?

Millie: Just do it, google Italian celebrity news, oh and make sure you click translate!

I do as she said and type the words into google making sure the translate is on, I click on the first site and I scroll down, there is what Millie is on about.

BREAKING NEWS: Italy's richest bachelor has been snagged!

The Billionaire Tripada Berluscioni has attended an event tonight with a very pretty young woman on his arm. I skip the rest of the words and scroll down and there I am in lots of photos; do I really look that good? Shows what an expensive dress and a team of beautifiers can do to a girl. Trip looks at my phone from over my shoulder,

"See model!" He teases and I give him a sarcastic look,

"Wait, isn't this bad with me not meant to be alive and all?" I whisper extra quietly; trip shakes his head.

"This won't reach London, especially not that prick anyway!" I come off the website and open my texts back up,

Me: That is nothing I am sat next to an actress who is trying to get her agent to sign me! I will explain everything later!

I put my phone back in my bag and continue enjoying the show, there's performances, awards, comedy and it has been quite fun so far.

"You come to afterparty? Si?" Viola asks and I look to Trip.

"Sorry, maybe next time." Trip answers politely with a smile before he can turn us to leave Camiellia hands me a card.

"Call me, Tomorrow?" I nod, but I have zero plans for calling her, I tuck the card into my purse and Trip leads us out of the venue. The paparazzi are still out front and we smile as the flashes start all over again, when we reach the car Trip opens the door for me and I slide in, he follows and as soon as he shuts the door the car starts to move.

"That is intense."

"The photographers? Yeah, they can be. I try and blend in public because they can hound you." He replies,

"Wait is that why you always have shades on when you dress all casual?" I ask, it clicking in my head and he nods. It does not take long to get home and as soon as we get out of the car Trip picks me up and puts me over his shoulders,

"Trip!" I squeal and he just laughs,

"I am not waiting for you to replay the whole night with Millie." Is the only response I get; he rushes through the foyer and up the stairs slamming our bedroom door open. When he puts me on the floor and looks me in the eyes all amusement has gone from both of us, the heat and connection that pulls me too him intensifies and when he kicks shut the door, I know a long night of torturous pleasure awaits me.

Chapter Sixteen

"I don't know about this Millie." I say as I wait to go onto the set.

"It's been Two weeks since the Gala and every agent in the city is after you, just do some test shots and see how you feel about it, you haven't decided on a job yet and this is a really big opportunity." I nod my head,

"Ok, yeah, your right, If I don't like it, I don't have to do it again." I say trying to steel my nerves.

"Exactly, so we have three costume changes, your more casual outfit, a sexy dress and a bikini." I go to the clothing rack and Millie hands me some Jeans, heels and a nice top with no back. I move behind the curtain and change, when I reappear, she smiles she comes over and touches up the makeup she has done on me and then leads me out into the studio. There are two or three different cameras' set up all facing the white background and floor, there are lots of different lights and I carefully walk around them.

"Hey, Skye Right?" The photographer comes over to me her hand outstretched. I nod and shake her hand. "I am Cara your photographer, don't worry about a thing, we will take some great test shots today." She smiles, she looks like she is in her mid-thirties and she has an American accent. "Ok, if you come stand here, we will get started." I move to the centre of the white floor where she is standing and she moves to the camera straight in front of me. She takes a few shots and plays around with it before nodding to herself. "Ok we will start easy." She says with a smile. "Hands above your head, bent elbows and turn your waist to the right slightly." The camera clicks a few times, "Ok now throw your head back, I do and I am told and try to stay as still as possible. Cara keeps giving me instructions and I keep following, after the clicks of the camera she smiles so I assume this is going well. Half an hour goes by and I find myself getting into this, "Ok, done! Take a break, get changed and we will get started on outfit two."

"So, how's she doing?" Millie asks and Cara just smiles,

"You can see for yourself later, all I am going to say is if you want to be a model, you're going to have no issues doing it." A grin spreads across Millie's face and mine copy's, I feel all the nerves disappear and excitement take its place. I go back into the changing room and grab a bottle of water before changing into the gold dress, it is really beautiful as all my clothes have been lately, I am going to turn into a brat if this carries on. Millie comes and does my hair, she pulls it out of the high ponytail it was in and lets the curls bounce down, she takes a piece of my hair from the side of my head plaiting it loosely and then pulls it over my head and turns it into a sort of headband, all my hair is now out of my face and it looks quite sweet. Millie adds some eyeshadow onto my makeup done but makeup free look and some lipstick,

"Perfect." She exclaims as she backs away from my chair so I can put my stilettos on. We head back out to the set and the lights aren't as bright for this section of the shoot. The poses Cara makes me do are a bit harder than before and she even comes over to move my limbs but once I know what she means I get it.

Soon I am all done, I felt a bit self-conscious when I had to put the white bikini on but with only Millie and Cara looking at me, I got more comfortable and I really did enjoy the whole day! I am now back into my normal clothes and Cara is showing us the Images.

"This one and this one are my favourites!" Cara exclaims as she pulls two photos up next to each other on her large computer screen.

"I see what you mean, Skye you look amazing." Millie states gleaming with pride, I study the first photo, it's one of me in the gold dress and I am laughing when I got the pose wrong and Cara captured the perfect moment. The other photo is when I am in the bikini, the background is black and my skin has glitter oil over it so I look wet and shiny. My face has a sultry look I didn't even know I had and my body is positioned so I look like I am just walking but it looks fucking hot, I barely recognise myself in these photos and I am really happy with how they turned out.

"I love them, all of them, you really do work magic with that camera!" I say to Cara and she just grins,

"That was all you. I won't need to photoshop anything, which makes you one of my favourite models already." Cara pulls me into a quick hug.

"Millie, I'll have these emailed over to you by tomorrow morning at the latest. Get in touch if you want to do some more shoots." She says as she starts to pack her stuff away.

"Do you need some help, packing up?" I ask her and she waves me off.

"My assistant will be here soon; he can do most of it." She winks and I chuckle, I am guessing by assistant she means husband if the ring on her finger is anything to go by. Once we exit the building our security is there and waiting for us, holding the car door open.

"I need to go to the office quickly, is that ok?" Millie asks,

"Of course." I smile because I can pop into see Trip while we are there.

When I step out of the car someone starts taking pictures of me, the security guy blocks me from the camera and hurries me into the building, he speaks to the guys on the security desk before taking me and Millie to the lifts and putting us in one. When we get out on the top floor it is surprisingly quite empty, it's dinner time and I assume most people are done for the day. Millie goes to her office which is the one closest to the lift and I head to Trip's. Matt looks up and smiles when he spots me,

"You not going home like everyone else?" I ask,

"Nah, got a few more things to do before I head out, I have the morning off tomorrow and I don't want to fall behind."

"Anything nice planned?"

"I am looking after my baby Niece for a while, my sister has got to go to work and the usual babysitter can't do tomorrow. It happens a lot but Trip is a good boss he lets me go as much as he can." I smile,

"Hey beautiful, what are you doing here?" Trip asks as he leans in the doorway of his office, Matt has already gone back to typing on his computer so I walk over to Trip, he kisses me before moving so I can enter his office.

"Millie needed to pop in, so here I am."

"How did the shoot go?" I turn to face him and I feel my face pale at the sight of his wall.

"What is that?" I point at the almost life-size photo of me, the one he took when I was sat in the kitchen in a ballgown.

"A Picture of my girlfriend, you don't like it." He is grinning the bastard.

"I like the photo yes. But really, it's like 5ft tall, do you really need a life-size picture of me on your office wall."

"I think I do. Yeah." Trip takes my face in his hands and kisses me gently. I almost forget about the photo but then he pulls back from me and it's right in my face again. "Anyway, if you're going to be a model, you're going to have to get used to it."

"I don't know if I even want to be a model!" I throw my hands in the air before dropping into his desk chair. Trip takes a seat on the actual desk,

"Did you not enjoy today?"

"Yeah, I did."

"Then do it, no one is making you do it forever, when you don't enjoy it anymore stop." I can't really think of anything to argue back with so I just open my mouth and close it again. "We have been through this, you don't even have to work if you don't want to, but you do. Why don't you just try modelling for a few months and see where it goes, we have looked at loads of other stuff and you don't want to do it." I nod my head,

"I know I am being a brat but I think you might be right, I'll give it a go, but I am not ever going to get used to seeing my picture everywhere!"

"You are not being a brat; I mean I couldn't decide what business I wanted to run so I bought loads of different ones." I laugh at his words, he certainly did. A knock at the door has us both turning to see Millie coming in followed by Tiao,

"I am done, ready to go?" She asks me and I nod, I press a quick kiss to Trip's lips before walking over to her,

"I'll take the girls home." Tiao tells Trip,

"Ok, we will be another hour or so." Trip states, "See you at home."

Chapter Seventeen
One month later

"SKYE!"

"Skye, over here."

"Skye, smile for us."

"Skye!" I walk down the street with Millie and we are being followed by what seems like hundreds of photographers, it's probably only a dozen but I can't see much apart from cameras in my face and the flashes are blinding me. I am trying to smile and let them take their pictures but they are not going away. Our two security guys are trying to help but it is proving futile. I have spent the past month doing shoots and working and life was feeling normal, I have my best friend, my boyfriend and Rina and the guys, it feels like my family but this... this is just out of this world. The Iceberg shoot I did a few weeks ago landed yesterday, the ads were everywhere, TV, billboards and every Italian magazine and now I am like some sort of celebrity.

"Let's duck in there, we can call Trip to come and save us." Millie smiles as though she is enjoying this, we go into the little café and our security lock the doors, explaining to the owner what's happening, they hand us both a coffee and I call Trip,

"Hey," He answers

"Hey, erm I need your help." I say on a half laugh,

"Why, what's happened, are you ok?"

"I am fine, it's just... Well, me and Millie wanted to go do a bit of shopping but now we are kind of stuck in a café with loads of reporters outside and we are trapped."

"Are you with your security?"

"Yeah, they're guarding the door." Trip laughs, like full on belly laughs.

"Ok, put one of them on." I pass the phone over and the guy speaks in Italian quickly, then hands the phone back to me.

"I am coming to save you." Trip teases,

"My hero." I reply sarcastically, Trip laughs again before hanging up. I take a seat and Millie follows suit.

"I think we should just stick to online shopping from now on." Millie chuckles and I roll my eyes,

"I can't even get my head around this! I mean look, more and more of them are turning up, I am not anything special!"

"Bitch, look at you! Your gorgeous young and talented, those pictures were off the chart, you look like a true pro. And add in that you have taken the most eligible bachelor in Italy of the market... They are going to want to take your picture and find out about you, your hot news." I roll my eyes at her. "It's going to get worse you know; another ad drops in a week and then two more drop the week after. You need to speak with your agent because I can't keep being the middleman too, I have heard Chanel want you for their perfume ad."

"Woah, Chanel, that's huge. Can I even do that, what if it gets back to London?"

"I don't know, you need to sort that out with Trip. He needs to do something, none of us expected you to blow up this fast, it only takes one reporter to dig up a little dirt on you and they will know your meant to be dead." She whispers the last part.

"Shit, I should have used a different name, or something."

"But what's the worst that can happen, Jay is not going to come here and challenge Trip, the guy is a pussy! Plus, he would get done for insurance fraud as you didn't know anything about it, and he got a fake body from somewhere."

"True! Maybe I should leak the story then, get there first, I mean it couldn't hurt right, like you said Jay can't get to me, the only reason we didn't out him before was because the plan was for me to go back to London and that is not happening now." Millie nods her head and we both sit there lost in our thoughts for a while. A load of shouting outside has me looking around Millie to see what's happening, a ton more reporters are here now and Trip is trying to get through them, eventually he does and our security let him in, he comes straight to me and pulls a chair from another table dragging it next to mine, he sits and kisses me kind of intensely.

"Are we not leaving?" Millie asked and I look from the crowd outside and Trip whose got a sheen of sweat on his forehead.

"We can't, he's trapped in here now too." I burst into laughter and so does Millie,

"So, what now?" Millie asks as she composes herself.

"Now, I get the superstar here more security for when she goes out and also the guys are coming up with a decoy." Trip steals my coffee and takes a sip before putting his arm around the back of my chair. I lean into his side and put my lips near his ear,

"We need to talk later."

"About what?" He sounds a bit worried

"I think I might need to rise from the dead." I lean back and raise an eyebrow and I see the tension ease from his shoulders, he gives me a half smile and nods. We sit and wait for what seems like forever but it's only fifteen minutes before all of the reporters check their phones and scurry away.

"Was that the decoy?" Millie asks and Trip just grins at her,

"What did they do?" I ask, Trip wiggles his eyebrows and I roll my eyes,

"Let's get out of here before they all come back." Trip asks and we haul arse back home.

We are all in the dining room chatting as we have just finished dinner, Luca helps Rina clear the table before coming back and retaking his seat.

"Skye, you said something earlier, about rising from the dead, what did you mean?" Trip asks, the whole room turns serious and all of their eyes are on me.

"Millie and I were talking about this earlier, none of us could have Imagined that I would be the object of the paparazzi's attention and not to this scale. There is a real possibility this could get back to London, or if a journalist digs a little, they could leak the story about me being, you know, dead!"

"So, what are you wanting to do?" Paul asks,

"I think I should be the one to leak the story, the whole story, just tweak the part of how I ended up here." I look around the table and everyone just stares at me, thinking about what I have just said, eventually the guys all nod.

THE BETTER MONSTER 113

"I think your right, the best outcome for you is for you to tell the story first, but I don't think we should do it in an Italian newspaper, we should go bigger." Tiao says,

"Get you on TV so people can hear it from you." Paul adds,

"Ok, here's what we're going to do." Trip says, taking charge. We spend the rest of the evening going over the plan, my story keeping everything truthful but how Trip got me here, I know exactly what to say and do, if I do this right, Jay will go down for insurance fraud as well.

⚜

FOUR DAYS LATER AND we are landing in New York, when Tiao said about going big, I didn't think he meant America big, but here we are! I go to the studio tomorrow morning and do my interview on Oprah to be aired the next day, then my agent has booked me in for a shoot in the afternoon. We all pile into the hotel suite and we all just drag ourselves to bed, it's late, we are all tired and I have to be up before the sun in the morning. I curl against Trip's side and rest my head on his chest.

"Are you ok with all of this; we can cancel if you decide not to do it."

"No, I want to do this, I am through with letting him win, I don't want all of this hanging over me. Anyway, everything else has been done, the police statement, the insurance company, this is the last step and I am finishing this!"

"Good." I feel his smile as he kisses my head. "Go to sleep, tomorrows going to be a long day." I lay there for ages trying to fall asleep, I hear Trip's breathing even out and I lay staring at the ceiling, I am fucking nervous! National American TV, that's going to end up worldwide, especially if Tiao has anything to do with it. Eventually I drift to sleep and thankfully a deep one.

"Turn it off!" I groan from under the pillow as Trip's alarm on his phone makes some ear-piercing sound.

"Get up and I'll turn it off, you have no time for snoozes today." I roll out of bed and land on my feet my eyes still shut, Trip chuckles and turns off the alarm. I crack open one eye and I am relieved when the room is still dark. I walk like a zombie to the bathroom and start getting ready. After I have showered and brushed my teeth, I walk back into the bedroom wrapped in a fluffy towel, I grab my clothes and put them on the end of the bed. Trip is sitting with his back against the headboard with a coffee and I join him. He passes me my own coffee and I blow on the steaming cup before taking a sip,

"Are you ready for today?" Trip asks and I shrug,

"I am ready to tell the story, but I don't think I am ready for the whole being on TV thing, I am only just becoming ok with seeing my face everywhere, being a model is still so new and I have no idea how to be famous, I don't know if I want to be famous at all."

"Babe, you're doing great, and you would have been famous either way, you're my girlfriend, it comes with the territory but at least now it's for your own achievements not mine."

"That's something else we need to talk about, you keep calling me your girlfriend, and telling everyone I am, but I never heard you ask me, and I certainly didn't ask you." I smile into my coffee cup,

"Oh really." Trip's eyebrow shoots up and I try to keep a straight face. Trip takes the mug from my hand and places it on his bedside table before coming closer to me. He puts his hands around my waist and lifts me up so I am straddling him, my towel amazingly stays in place. His hands grip my hips tightly and he put his face so close to mine. "Skye, do you want to be my Girlfriend, officially?" His voice is deep and sexy and it sends shivers down my spine. I shrug and his eyes go wide, his hand goes in my towel and then he is tickling me, I thrash around on his lap, laughing so hard I can barely talk.

"Please...Trip...Stop!" He doesn't instead he flips us over so my back in flat on the mattress and he's over me, my towel finally relented and now I am naked, he uses both hands to tickle me now and I can barely breathe. My hands land on his shoulders and my nails dig into his muscles. The moment of fun and laughter suddenly changes to serious and my skin heats as he looks into my eyes with adoration in them. "I want to be your Girlfriend, officially." I whisper, a wide grin spreads across his face, making him look the fun, sweet guy that not many people know lives inside of him. Trip crushes my mouth with his and his tongue darts into my mouth, my hand goes into his hair and my legs wrap around his waist. I feel his dick harden and I moan into his mouth as it rubs against me. Trip puts mor of his weight on me as one hand that was holding him above me trails down my side until he finds what he is looking for. He groans into my mouth when he feels how wet I am for him and I whimper as he plunges two fingers into me, curling them so I arch my back. I reach for his sweats and push them down, freeing his cock which is rock hard for me, he moves so he is kneeling in-between my legs, grabs my hips and pulls me down the bed before lifting one of my legs and placing it on his shoulder. Trip lowers and kisses me again, his cock is at my entrance and I wiggle down so his tip is in me, Trip chuckles before he thrusts hard and I swear to god I see stars. My back arches off the bed and my hands grip his sides as he kisses my now exposed neck. I am moaning and writhing under him as he thrusts into me, hitting the right spots over and over, his teeth sink into my shoulder as my nails rake down his back as we come together, the room fills with screams and groans until all we can hear is both of us panting. Trip lifts his head from where he was resting it by my own and kisses me sweetly.

Chapter Eighteen

I am sat in a very comfy armchair in the middle of the Oprah studio with some girl in a headset telling me what's going to happen, I am so nervous as I stare out into the audience who are all taking their seats, I take some deep breaths and remind myself of why I have to this, why I need to claim my own life back. Oprah walks onto the set with a massive round of applause, she smiles to the audience and waves as she makes her way over to me, I stand and we shake hands before both taking our seats.

"Skye, it's lovely to meet you. How are you feeling?"

"Nervous." I give her a small smile and she nods her head.

"I have read your story and I would be nervous too but you're doing the right thing, doing this will not only set yourself free but also set others who are still stuck free too." I nod my head and that information just makes me even more determined to do this and do this right! After a few moments someone from the crew counts down from five and then I hear someone yell rolling.

"Hello, we are here today to listen to a young woman's harrowing story of domestic violence, a story that she has never told anyone fully and with this she hopes to finally get her freedom. Skye Brackwell has not long turned Twenty-One and has been trapped in an abusive relationship for six years, the worst thing about this story is how even though through a chance meeting she finally escaped she is still not free." Oprah turns to me her face is kind but serious, this is it. "Skye, how did you find yourself in such a traumatic relationship and so young?"

"We met when I was fourteen and he was sixteen, we went to the same school, I was year nine and he was year eleven, we hung out in similar crowds had mutual friends and used to see each other all the time. At first, we started talking, mainly through text and this went on for a year, we were just close friends. He was sweet, kind, and funny and I used to get excited whenever he texted me, after about a year, he had finished school and our texting slowed to pretty much never. I saw him at a house party one night and we had a laugh, like normal people do and then he kissed me. We were more serious over the next couple of months and then we were official, and exclusive. I didn't see any signs of what I was in for, no red flags, nothing. Fast forward a year and I am doing my exams to finish school; my mum and dad didn't like Jay and we had a huge fight over it. Jay convinced me to move out and move into his flat with him, I was stupid and young and I thought I was in love so I did. I have not spoken to my parents from that day, they cut me out completely.

"Do you know why your parents did that?"

"No, we had a great, loving relationship before Jay, but I didn't do anything to upset them, I knew they didn't like him, they never told me why but they turned on me so fast."

"So, what happened next."

"The control! Soon enough Jay was ordering me around, shouting in my face if I didn't do something, he had told me to do. I was now a live-in maid, not a girlfriend. He stopped me from going to college after school was over and he would only let me apply for jobs he had picked out. My friends list got shorter and shorter, I was not allowed to speak to anyone, the only friend I had was my lifelong best friend Millie, who he couldn't pluck from life even though he tried, she is tenacious." I smiled and Oprah chuckled.

"Did Millie know about all of this."

"No, I kept it from her, I didn't want her involved so I made excuses." Oprah nodded her head. "When I had been living there about eight months, the beatings started. This went on up until the day I got out. I was controlled, beaten and almost broken."

"You took photos didn't you, of the bruises he left on your body."

"Yeah, I kept evidence with time stamps on, I needed something I could use if I ever went to the police or evidence for the police to use if he killed me. The thing when you are so stuck is you know one day he will do it, he will go too far."

"I am going to show the photos, please be aware this footage is not appropriate for children." Oprah looks behind us where the big screen is and a gasp leaves the audience. I watch as pictures of me roll on and off the screen, one after the other showing all the different bruises on my skin. We watch for a good five minutes in silence the odd gasp from the audience, the bruises get worse over time and then finally Oprah looks back to me. "We couldn't show them all, as there was over Three Thousand photos documenting your abuse. But there is one in particular I wanted to show next." We both look up at the screen and I see myself in the hospital with a broken leg, a bandage around my head and bruises everywhere. "What happened this time."

"I tried to escape; I was about eighteen. I ran, I made it out of London and into a hotel, but he found me, easily and dragged me into the back of the car, he then crushed my leg with his foot and used his hand to bend it so it broke, he then caved my head in by slamming it over and over again into the car door."

"How did you feel after that incident?"

"I didn't really feel anything, the only emotion I had was angry. I just lost all hope, I went through my days just waiting for him to kill me off, it was a strange emotion to feel, it was like I had already let go of my soul and just didn't care anymore, I hardly ever fought him back, I stopped begging for him to stop, I didn't live, I existed."

"What happened the day you got away?" Oprah prompted,

"I went to work, came back and Jay was getting ready, he had told me he was taking me out with him that night as it was my Twenty-First birthday, and when I mentioned it, he went on one, he gave the usual emotional abuse, the name calling, telling me how embarrassing and worthless I am. Then he beat me, I was left on the floor of the hallway with probably a broken rib. The thing was he knew where to punch and kick so no one would ever know, his rep, his life everything would be ruined if people knew and he knows it. Millie called me asking where he was taking and me and when I told her, he had gone out without me, she did not take no for an answer, she was at the flat putting me in a dress and dragging me to a club."

"Millie sounds like a great friend."

"I am!" Millie's shouts from the audience, I look over to see her with tears rolling down her face. The boys are sat next to her and they all look furious. Trip looks like he is about to murder someone. Oprah chuckles at Millie and turns back to me, nodding so I can continue.

"I Smoke when I have had a few drinks, I just get the craving. I left Millie by the bar and went to the smoking area at the back of the club. I spotted Jay in a booth surrounded by his friends and a barely dressed girl grinding on his lap. I know he saw me so I just kept walking, I was sat outside when a guy in a suit came and sat next to me and asked me for a cigarette. We talked for a bit and the conversation I had with him made me want to leave, I planned to go back in the club, tell Millie everything and get all my stuff before Jay got back and I would be gone."

"But?"

"But I couldn't find her, I looked everywhere and was stood in the ladies' bathroom, when Jay pounced. He head-butted me and broke my nose, which is still healing! And then he put something over my mouth and nose which basically knocked me out. The next thing I know is I am waking up in a big mansion in Italy."

"How did you end up there?"

"The guy that I spoke to in the smoking area, his name is Trip and after our conversation he came looking for me, to buy me a drink I think he said. Then he overheard Jay on the phone as he walked past the bathrooms, Jay had told someone, she was ready and that he would bring her out. Trip thought it sounded odd and when Jay left the bathroom with me over his shoulder, drugged and bloody, he knew I wasn't being carried to safety. Trip went out of a side door and raced around the club to the carpark. He leaned against his car and waited; sure, enough Jay rounded the corner with me. Jay didn't even question who he was, he just handed me over with my passport and told him he expected his money in twenty-four hours. Trip asked in a douche bag way how much I was worth and Jay told him. Sixty Thousand pounds, he also let a big hint slip when he was walking away, Jay said The Mexicans can rent the bitch out for all I care. Trip put me in his car and strapped me in, he waited around for the guy who was meant to get me, soon enough he showed and Trip managed to get him to call his boss, he offered him Two hundred and fifty grand plus the sixty that still needed paying to Jay. They accepted and they also accepted the terms that Jay was never to know."

"So, Trip bought you instead?"

"Yeah, So I woke up and I thought I had been kidnapped, Trip explained to me what had happened and thought it was best to bring me to Italy, where no one would recognise me. Trip offered to set me up anywhere in the world when I was ready, he looked after me, got doctors in to look at my injuries, made sure I ate, took me shopping, made me do things to figure out what I liked to do for fun and even offered me a job at one of his companies. Don't get me wrong I had my doubts, I was spending so much time with him and catching some hardcore feelings, but something always niggled at me in the back of my mind, I always just thought what if I was meant to be sold to him."

"And what changed."

"The day he flew me back to London and put a wig on me, I had to attend my own funeral, I sat upstairs watching my best friend cry, Jay and his mate laugh and my dad just looking sad. My mum was not even there! I had asked him if I could see Millie and even though it could cause trouble for me, he made it happen, we got her and her stuff and she didn't hesitate to get on that plane and move to Italy for me. From that I knew he was helping me and had no reason to hurt me, he was just at the right place at the right time."

"So why are you here telling your story today?"

"Jay faked my death to claim on life insurance I didn't even know I had, and I don't want to be looking over my shoulder for the rest of my life, I have found a career and I like it but I can't do it to my full potential."

"Modelling?" A few pictures go across the screen of my modelling so far.

"Yeah, I have had some big brands approach me, but if I did them, he would see them as they would be advertised worldwide. I don't know if he would come after me but I do not want to even give him that option. When this goes live tomorrow, he will have nowhere to hide, everyone will know what he did and I can live my life however I want to."

"Have the police been informed."

"They have, but I don't know if they will do much. I just want to forget him, move forward with my life and live it however I want."

"You are so brave and strong Skye, and I sincerely hope you have the life you deserve. Do you have any messages for other women out there in the same situations you were." I look dead into the camera and take a deep breathe.

"Tell someone, everyone, you have nothing to be ashamed for what he does, you can get out, but you will need someone to help you. You can win just like I have."

Chapter Nineteen

I wake up to the sound of someone calling my name and I groan, we only got home last night and I am not ready to wake up.

"Skye, mio povero amico, dove sei?" The Italian voice gets louder,

"Is that Viola?" Trip asks and I chuckle,

"I think it is, what did she say?"

"My poor friend, where are you?" Trip translates. I get out of bed and throw on one of Trip's T-shirts, it comes to my mid thighs so I am decent enough. I walk out the bedroom door and follow her voice to the kitchen where she is now having a conversation in Italian with Rina.

"Viola? What are you doing here?" I ask with a smile and she practically runs to me in the kitchen doorway and wraps me in a hug.

"I saw the show, and I had to come and see you! You poor thing." She pulls back and eyes me from head to toe. "Magnifico, even in the morning!" She says and I shake my head as I chuckle, I move over to Rina who is holding out a coffee for me and I thank her as I take a seat. Trip walks in and Viola pounces on him. "Grande uomo! You are a hero, saving this beautiful girl." Trip looks like a dear in headlights and I hold back a laugh as Viola pulls him in for a hug too. "Sit, have coffee, Camiellia will be here in a minute, she has big news for you Skye." She takes a seat beside me and Trip rounds the counter to stand with Rina. Viola speaks to Trip and Rina in Italian and I zone out while I drink my coffee. Camiellia is escorted into the kitchen by one of the guards and she looks like she has just won the lottery or something. She places her tablet and phone on the vacant spot beside me and says her hellos to everyone before taking the seat.

"Skye, you are a hot commodity, since the show aired yesterday, I have had calls and emails constantly. Everyone wants you; we have a solid Calendar of work for at least six months!"

"Seriously?"

"Yes, all the big brands want you, Perfume, clothes, make-up, runways and charity's at least thirty domestic violence charity's all over the world want you to be their ambassador."

"Right, Well, what now?"

"Now I go through all of them and organise your schedules. Is there anyone you don't want to work with?"

"No, I can work with everyone."

"I need access to her calendars and I will put you in contact with my team to organise transport, she must have security with her." Trip tells Camiellia and she nods.

"I am going to hire you a team of people, hair and makeup, people to dress you in the right clothes, personal shoppers, assistant the lot. You are being thrust into the deep end here but your team can help you through it. Take the weekend to relax and prepare, Monday will the start of a very busy six months."

"How was it?" Trip asks as I step into his office at home, late Monday evening.

"Crazy! I now have like fifteen people who will follow me around all day like little puppy dogs." Trip laughs as he pulls me onto his lap, I wrap my hands around his neck and kiss him long and hard.

"Did you have to do any work?" I shake my head,

"Just had meetings, mainly going through schedules, meeting people that now work for me, going through some of the contracts and stuff like that, I do have to leave in the middle of the night though. My first shoot is in Paris, Chanel want me to do a photo shoot and a TV ad." I show Trip how nervous I am and runs his finger over the crease in my forehead.

"You will be perfect, as always. You will be so busy and having so much fun you won't even miss me." He teases and I pout.

"Can't you come with me?"

"Nah, baby. I have an Important meeting I can't push back, plus it's only until Wednesday lunchtime, I will take you out for dinner when you get home."

"Okay," I said giving him a smile. "I am going to play zombies for a bit." I say as I wiggle out of his lap and go to the living room. "Pass me one of those." I say as I drop down beside Tiao, he hands me a controller and adds me into his party so I can start playing.

"Fuck, revive me please, I got trapped!" He says in annoyance as I round up the Zombies and run straight for him, I revive him quickly before we both sprint off only looking back to shoot every now and again. I pick up a Semtex bomb and throw it at the hoard of zombies behind me killing half of them and giving me enough essence to open a door. I run through it and buy the gun on the wall before turning back and shooting more zombies. After ten or so rounds we both die and I can't be bothered to play again so I wave bye to Tiao and head up to bed.

After hours of shooting the TV ad, which to my utter shock went really well, I am now standing in front of the Eiffel Tower holding Chanel's newest perfume in a white billowy dress.

"That's a wrap!" The Photographer says with a wide smile.

"That's it?"

"That is, it, you were perfect and we have everything we need and more." He says as he starts packing away his equipment. I walk towards my assistant, Rose, as she scrolls through her phone.

"Hey, so what next?"

"Well, you have a bit of free time now, you will need to start getting ready for the Chanel party at Six so you have a few hours to kill."

"Can I nap?" I ask with a laugh and she nods,

"Can you get changed first; I think Em wants to do a few shots for Instagram." I rush to change in the hotel which is located just across the road and within fifteen minutes I am changed and Em is taking some shots of me out in the streets of Paris, I have a huge grin on my face which is genuine and I feel so different today, I feel finally, completely free, I have no worries on my shoulders and no stress to care about. With everything going so well this morning my anxiety over modelling has faded to nothing and I can feel my confidence just growing. After an hour of taking photos with Em I head up to my hotel room, which of course is a massive, luxurious room! I decided a nap would be useless now, but I did have time to watch a movie and stuff my face with popcorn, I landed on the princess diaries and laid on the bed while I laughed at a young Anne Hathaway finding out she is a princess. My phone starts dinging on the bed next to me and I look at the screen which shows notification after notification. I click on the top one and it takes me to my Instagram account which is blowing up! Em had put the account on my phone so I could post if I wished to, I scroll down my profile at the pictures he took and I must say the guy has skills! Comments and likes are reaching the thousands on each photo and they have only just been posted! The banner at the top of my screen says @TripBerlusciono has just commented on your photo, I click the banner and it takes me to a photo where I am smiling as I look up at the Eiffel Tower. The comment from Trip says

The most beautiful thing I have seen all day. **red heart emoji**. *I* reply

Grinning face emoji *Your so biased. I* smile as I put the phone down and just chill watching the film until I have to get ready.

Chapter Twenty

"Are you sober enough to go do some night-time shots?" Em asks as we exit the lift on our floor,

"Yeah, I only had a couple, give me twenty minutes to put the other dress on." I reply as I swipe my key card in the door.

"Okay, see you in a mo." I pull out my phone as I kick the door shut and check my notifications, which there are thousands of, due to the never-ending likes and comments on Instagram. I don't see anything from Trip or Millie, so I put it down on the ironing board I forgot to put away earlier and head to the bedroom. I scream when I enter the dark room and a hand grabs me another hand going across my mouth to muffle the sound. My breathing gets shallow as I start to panic, I am dragged backwards as I struggle against whoever is gripping me. I am spun around quickly and I come face to face with Jay, Shit! How did he get to me, he should be in prison by now.

"What do you want Jay?" I spit as I try to back up, his fist collides with my cheek and my head snaps to the side with the force of it.

"You really are a stupid bitch, you think I wouldn't come after you, after you boosted yourself up in the world by making me a fucking monster and losing me a huge payday." Another punch to my face has my head spinning a bit and I stumble as I try to stay upright, fear tries to worm its way back in. I am done being scared; I am done letting him think he is winning.

"Your actions did that to you, not me." I say with much more calm than I expected, Jay punches me again and I lose my balance and end up on the floor, Jay kicks me before he leans down next to me grabbing my hair and tugging my hair back.

"How long before your scummy arse slept with your kidnapper, huh?" I ignore him and he pulls harder making me hiss out a breath of pain. "Your nothing but a whore, I bet he had you before you even got off the plane!" He pushes my head with all of his force and the side of it smashes against the floor, Jay gets up and I try to stand but I can't, I start to crawl, trying to get away. I let out a scream of pain and tears fall from my eyes as something hits my back hard making me sprawl out flat on the floor, my cheek is flat to the floor and I see the folded-up ironing board come down onto my back again. I cry out after every hit; I feel bones break and the wet sticky blood coat my skin where the ironing board smashes into me over and over and over again. This is it, this is the moment I waited for, after all those years of beatings, this is where he finally kills me. The pain stops as my whole body goes numb, the tears lessen as I lay motionless on the ground, I hear him grunt and the sound the ironing board makes as it hits me but everything else just stops and it's just me in my head in these last moments. I hear the crash as he throws the board across the room, he leans down so his face is just above mine.

"You are going to die, and I couldn't be happier about it but before you do, let's cut that pretty face of yours, make you ugly in your final moments." Jay sneers. I see the knife as he presses down into my cheek hard with it, he slices down and

I scream as the pain comes back. I feel the blood pour down my face and some even gets in my eye making me see everything through a red tint. Jay smiles as he gets up and I hear him laugh just before the door slams closed behind him. I close my eyes as I go numb again and I accept that I will die here. This was my fate all along, to be murdered by that monster. Flashes of Millie, Trip and the guy's flit across my mind and silent tears mesh with the blood dripping down my face. I finally had a family and he got to take it away. He can't take how happy they made me though. I love them, all of them and I wish I got the chance to tell them. My phone rings from the floor and I turn my head to see it, it takes me a lot of effort and I clench my teeth through the pain that assault's me again. It's not far, I can get to it. I try to get on my hands and knees but I fail, the pain to unbearable, I stretch my hand out and use my foot to slide me slowly across the floor. I finally manage to touch it with my fingertips and I drag it to me. The face ID does not work from this position and maybe because the state of my face so I fumble as I enter my password, after two attempts I get it. I use my finger to scroll down to Trip's name as the phone lays just in front of me flat to the floor. I press call and instantly put it on speaker as I let my head fall back to the floor, my energy is almost non-existent and black and white dots are blurring my vision. Please answer, I haven't got long. The ring tone seems to go on and off for a lifetime but finally he answers.

"Hey, you back at the hotel?" Trip asks, I go to talk but cough instead, blood flies out of my mouth spotting the floor and I take a large breath.

"I am sorry." My voice is hoarse and so quiet. "I couldn't stop him." I cough again, expelling more blood.

"Skye, are you ok? What happened." His tone is suddenly worried, deeper, and darker than before.

"Jay," I cough some more, "He found me, I don't have long." I cough worse this time and I have to shut my eyes as the room spins too much.

"Where are you? what did he do to you? I am texting your team, they will help you, just stay calm baby." I can hear the panic in his voice,

"I love you Trip! Tell the others bye for me."

"No. You keep your eyes open, Rose is on her way to you, just stay awake, baby, help is coming." I hear banging on the door and shouting coming from Rose and Em, but it's too late. I cough some more and I feel myself slipping, the darkness taking over all I can hear as I struggle to stay in this world is Trip shouting down the phone for me to stay awake.

Chapter Twenty-One

All I can see is darkness, I don't feel anything, I can't look around I am Immobile staring into the blackness, I don't know if I am dead or alive but I keep hearing voices echoing through the black fog and It's driving me mad.

"She's been out for weeks, look at her! This is my fault!" Trip's voice reaches me, he sounds so sad and so very desperate that makes me believe I am still alive but I can't wake up, I can't do anything but listen to snippets of conversation and stare at this black fog that has taken over my mind.

"Miss Brackwell's chances of waking up are getting smaller with each day that passes, we don't know what level of brain damage she has, you may want to think about turning the machines off."

"No, you have said before she may not have any brain damage, she will wake up, she just needs time!" Trip's voice booms and I can feel his rage, but I do need to wake up, I just don't know how.

I try everything to get out of this black hole I seem to be stuck in but nothing happens, I finally give up, I know I am not getting out of this cage my own brain has locked me into, I think about all the good things in my life and even though I can't picture anything I smile or I think I do anyway. Then I think of everything that led me here, all the abuse, all the moments I could have got away but didn't and then I think of what is probably my last night awake, walking into that room and not knowing what was happening. All of a sudden, I feel burning hot rage consume me and colours speed past as I am thrown into the memory of Jay trying to kill me, I am standing to the side as I watch him smash that ironing board into me over and over. I watch the light fade from my own eyes, the fight leave's me and it fuels my rage even more. Suddenly I am thrown back and I feel like I have been thrown at a force for miles, my body soaring in the air, colours of my memories zoom past me in a blur and then within a split second everything stops as I jolt and I open my eyes to see a white ceiling and bright white lights hurting my eyes.

I slowly realise that I am awake, really awake, I try and sit up, it takes me a while but I manage it, I look over to the side of my bed and just stare at Trip. His forehead is creased, his fashionable stubble is now out of control and I can see the dark circles under his eyes. I cough and I soon realise I need some water, the pain hits me then but not where I expect, my neck and throat feel like there on fire, I cough again and Trip's beside me in an instant.

"Oh my god!" He presses a button that is by my bed and nurses rush into the room. One of them claps her hand over her mouth before running right back out, that's weird right? I am disorientated as people squeeze parts of my body, shine lights into my eyes and ask me a ton of questions. A guy comes into the room and clears his throat and everyone stops what they are doing and the room goes calm. The nurses hand the doctor pieces of paper before they all leave, Trip comes over and holds a glass of water and a straw out so I can have a sip, he puts it down when I have had enough and takes my hand holding it tight.

"Good news Miss Brackwell, everything seems normal so far. Can you remember what happened to you?" The doctor asks as he walks closer to the bed. I swallow the lump in my throat before nodding.

"Good, there seems to be no sign of any long-term effects of your injuries or the coma but notify someone straight away if you get any intense head pain, you can't remember things or feel you have any gaps in your memory. Your throat will be painful for a few days as you had a tube down it to help you breath so it's a bit bruised, normal pain killers should ease any discomfort. Do you have any questions for me? any pain? Any concerns?"

"I, erm..." My voice is barely there and it makes my throat itch like crazy when I talk, "How long have I been in a coma?" I ask,

"A Little over a month, you will need to continue to rest, being in a coma is very exhausting for your body so you will feel tired and will need to sleep, but I suggest you try and eat before sleeping now." I nod, Trip walks over to the doctor and shakes his hand before coming right back to my side, he perches on the bed and I only just realise most of the wires have disappeared from my body, those nurses are quick! Trip stares at me for a while and there is an awkward silence between us, he runs his hand through his hair,

"Skye, I am so fucking sorry!" Trip says and my eyes go wide,

"What for, you did nothing wrong." I start coughing and he grabs the water for me again, he rubs my back as I take small sips through the straw. "This is not your fault!" I look up at him hoping he can see how much I mean that!

"I just... I should have been there, you should have had more security, I should..."

"Stop! This is not your fault at all! No amount of precautions would have stopped him! I don't need you feeling guilty." Trip looks into my eyes and I can see him lose his guilt I see him doing what I need him to do and it makes my heart race. He smiles at me,

"What do you need?"

"Right now, I need to get out of this bed, and I need a shower!"

"Ok!" Without hesitating Trip lifts me into his arms, I take the device off my finger and he slowly puts my feet on the floor, I lean on him as we slowly walk to the bathroom, Trip puts me on the counter while he runs a bath for me and I slowly get down and take a look in the mirror. I look so skinny, my skin is dull and my eyes look lifeless, I pick at the corner of the big bandage that covers my left cheek, I slowly pull it down and I drop it on to the counter. I gasp as I stare at the huge scar that runs from just below my eye to just above my mouth, it is curved out so it is bigger than I thought it would be. I look away from the mirror and try not to let the tears fall, I was almost dead and this is what gets me the most emotional a fucking scar! Trip takes me in his arms and turns me to face him and I feel so embarrassed, he tips my head up to look at me and he smiles sweetly. Trip's finger comes up and he gently traces it over the bumpy scar.

"This does not affect how utterly beautiful you are, the scar will fade and be less noticeable but it will always be a part of you, a reminder of how strong you are and the demons you have had to face to be here today and that adds to your beauty!" I can see he means every word but I don't agree this scar just joins all of invisible ones that live inside me, it makes me broken and weak, and that is exactly what I am, a broken girl that can't get away from the monsters and I am too weak to face them and win. Trip guides me over to the bath and helps me get the awful hospital gown off before helping me sink into the warm, inviting bubbles. He sits on the floor beside the bath, his forearms rest on the rim as he stares into my face. I pull my knees up and rest my head on them shutting my eyes. "I never thought I would see you again, and then I thought you wouldn't wake up, I have never felt pain like it. I never got the chance to tell you that I love you, I thought I had lost you forever." I open my eyes to see him still staring at me and I give him a small smile,

"I love you too and I thought the same, I thought that was the end for me and now I am not sure what is next, he is never going to stop coming for me and I am so angry, at him, the world at myself and I just can't seem to see a way out of this cycle." Trip leans forward and presses a kiss to my forehead that sends warmth into me and leaves my skin tingling,

"We will figure this all out, we will get rid of him, if it's the last thing I do," He sighs and moves to the end of the bath. "Lean back babe." I do as he tells me and lean my head back on the end of the bath and relax into the water. Water is poured carefully onto my hair before fingers massage shampoo into my head making me relax even more, the vanilla scent of the shampoo filling my nose, I get lost in this moment memorising it, keeping it safe, just in case.

Chapter Twenty-Two

I wake up feeling less drained and disoriented this time, Trip is sat next to me and smiles when I look at him, he passes me a bottle of water as I sit up.

"How long was I asleep?"

"A few hours, the doctor has given the ok for me to take you home. I can get a hotel until you are up for the flight." I shake my head,

"We're still in France?"

"Yeah, I didn't want to move you, I thought it would be best for you to stay here."

"Oh, erm I want to just go home, I can handle a small flight." I stare into his eyes and he looks between mine searching for the truth in my words and he must see it.

"Ok, eat something I'll get it sorted, we will be home in a couple of hours." Trip gets up and pulls out his phone, texting quickly before leaving the room. I soon realise this the first time He's left me alone since I have woken up and I start to panic, I look around the room and brace myself for someone to jump out, my breathing quickens and I feel so helpless and it makes me angry at the same time. Hot stream of tears start to fall down my face and I curl myself into a ball and attempt to think about something else, try to snap myself out of this paranoia, but it's hopeless. I feel how scared I am by the way my whole-body shakes and I hate it; the door opens, I jump, and a sob escapes my throat.

"Shit! Skye, baby what's happened?" Trip runs around the bed and kneels beside it so I am face to face with him, my arms grab for him instantly and I am not sure if I jumped on him or he pulled but I am in his arms, wrapped tightly around him.

"I, I can't be alone." I squeak, Trip's shoulders drop and he releases a breath. He holds me tighter and my fear and paranoia start to disappear.

"Sorry, baby, I didn't think. I am here you are not alone ok." I nod into the crook of his neck and he rubs soothing circles into my back. "Let's go home.

I wake up with so much energy today, like a normal amount of energy, I don't feel drained or ill anymore. We have been home a week and I have slept for most of that Trip never leaving me like he promised, but today I am up, showered and dressed and ready to face life. I haven't seen Millie, Rina or the guys, Trip gave them strict orders and I heard Millie arguing with Taio the other night about it. Trip is still sleeping as I walk out the bedroom and shut the door. I don't feel as scared here, this is my home and I don't feel the earth-shattering paranoia like I did at the hospital. I walk into the kitchen and Rina is there making coffee and breakfast like normal and it makes me smile, she looks up and she gasps when she sees me, she practically sprints round he counter and envelopes me in a tight hug, which I return.

"Mia dolche ragazza!"

"English Rina." I chuckle, she pulls back and briefly cups my face her eyes watery and shining with affection.

"Come, sit. I make you coffee!" I do as she says and she whips around the kitchen before placing a steaming coffee in front of me and my god it smells amazing. I hear Millie's voice echo through the house as she tells someone exactly how pissed she is,

"No, she is my best friend and I should be able to see her, she's been home for a week and I have been barred from even popping my head in the door!"

"I get that but Trip is just looking out for her, she needs her..." Tiaos words trail off as they both enter the kitchen and spot me, I am smirking just because it feels appropriate at this point. Millie runs at me and nearly knocks me off the stool with the mammoth hug she gives me.

"I have been so worried!" She whispers in my ear her voice cracking, I pull back and smile at her,

"I am ok, I was just tired." Tiao pats my shoulder as he walks past us to sit on a stool.

"Good to have you home, Skye. We have all missed you and that one has been driving everyone crazy without you!" I chuckle and Millie shrugs her shoulder, taking a seat of her own.

"I am taking the day off; I am going to spend some much-needed time with my bestie!" Millie announces and I chuckle.

"I see you're feeling better." Trip walks in the kitchen followed by Paul and Luca, he comes over an places a sweet kiss on my forehead before taking his seat next to me. Paul nods his head in my direction and Luca ruffles my hair as he walks past. Everyone starts to chat to each other about work, they all fill Trip in on what he's missed at the office, I drift into a blank stare, no longer hearing what the others are saying, my thoughts go to where they always go lately, I see flashes of his face, the ironing board and the blood, the fear and the rage hits me at full force but I don't move I don't make a sound, I just keep it inside of me and hope it stays there.

"Skye!" Millie says, nudging my arm, I snap out of the trance I was in and Immediately smile, it's not real, I don't feel like smiling but I can't worry anyone more than I have already.

"Sorry, got lost in a daydream." I reply on a chuckle,

"What do you want to do today, just me and you? Shopping and a nice lunch?" I gulp at her suggestion and before I. can say anything Trip shoots her down

"I don't think it's a good idea for Skye to be going out just yet She's still recovering." I am just about to let relief fill me but I watch as Millie's eyes fill with sadness,

"No, I want to go, I need to face the world and get back to normal, a few hours shopping isn't going to kill me Trip."

"Are you sure?" I can see him scanning my face for any hint that I don't want to go so I plaster a reassuring smile on my face and give him a nod. "Ok then but take Paul with you and I'll arrange a security team." I roll my eyes at him like I normally would, but I do feel much better knowing we are going to be surrounded by a mean team of gang members who won't let anyone near us.

I AM BASICALLY DRAGGED out the front door by Millie as she had her arm looped inside of mine, I chuckle at her huge smile, and it pushes back some of the fear I had when I stood just staring out the door a minute ago. She lets go of my arm and slides in the car, I walk around to the other side and have to take some deep breaths, my hand shakes violently as I reach for the car door handle and it seeing it makes me so angry that I rip the door open and slam it one I am inside, Paul gives me a strange look through the windscreen mirror, and I make myself look away. We soon arrive at the shopping centre that Millie wanted to go and the car stopping pulls me out of my own head which again is keeping me in an endless circle of rage and fear by making me watch flashbacks of my attack, but they seem to be getting worse each time, like it's more dragged out the pain is more and the sounds much louder. I shake my head and quickly follow the others out of the car.

"Are you ok?" Paul asks as we follow Millie into the centre,

"Yeah fine." I smile and quickly catch up to Millie, Paul knows I am not ok and I really don't need him telling Trip so I need to fake being my normal self-much better!

"You have to try this on!" Millie shoves a long-fitted dress into my arms and shoves me towards the changing rooms. I make quick work of stripping off and putting the dress on, I must admit it is gorgeous, but I have lost a bit of weight since everything, and it looks weird hanging off me like that.

"Hey, Millie?"

"Yeah?" She says through the curtain

"Can you grab me a size smaller, this one's a bit big."

"Sure!" I stare in the mirror, and I catch sight of the big scar down my face even through the layers of foundation that I used to cover it, a tear falls, and I watch it as my body freezes with fear.

"You are going to die, and I couldn't be happier about it but before you do, let's cut that pretty face of yours, make you ugly in your final moments." Jay sneers. I see the knife as he presses down

into my cheek hard with it, he slices down so slowly, and I can feel it going in deep I hear my own scream as the excruciating pain radiates through me. I feel the sticky blood pour down my face and some even gets in my eye making me see everything through a red tint. Jay smiles wickedly and that's all I can see that evil man with his proud wicked smile."

A hand touches my shoulder and I snap, I don't see or hear anything but my own anger, I hit out again and again, screaming as I do, I just keep hitting, kicking and throwing anything I can get my hands on, I am suddenly pushed against the wall and I hear a muffled voice shouting. I struggle against the person holding me, but they won't budge, eventually after what feels like hours, I hear Paul's voice calmly telling me to breathe, I do and finally I calm down, I snap my eyes open and gasp when I see the changing room, the curtain is ripped down and there are bits of mirror all over the floor. There's blood smeared on some shards too and I look down at my hands my knuckles are cut to shreds. Paul releases me and I sink to the ground and start to cry,

"Who did I hurt?" I say through hiccups of sobs,

"Mostly me, but the shop assistant got a punch to the nose." He says as he sits down in front of me.

"I am so sorry!" The crying intensifies, and I don't know how to stop the tears. Paul sits there patiently in front of me until I eventually stop crying enough to function a bit.

"Listen, I know you're not ok and if I had to guess, your constantly thrown back to your attack and you only feel pure anger at the world right now." I nod, "You have PTSD Skye, and it won't just go away, most people see a therapist, but I have a feeling that is not the solution here!" I look up into Paul's eyes and I can see his own pain as he swallows before talking again. "I went through a lot as a child, I was beaten, chained up for days on end, abandoned and forced to do things no child should ever go through, in face no adult should either. When I got away in my teens I saw a therapist, four actually, but talking about my shit did not help at all, in fact it made it worse. When I met Trip and the others it started to get better, but it never went away, I pushed it aside for so many years the one day it all just hit me and I didn't know what to do, Trip found me trying to hang myself in our dorm room."

"Paul, you don't..."

"I do, I have to help you now, so you don't get to that point."

"How can you help me? Look at what I just did!"

"Trip sent me to this place, it's not that far from here, I stayed there and trained for over a year, and they taught me everything I know today, from fighting to guns to mental health and how to deal with my emotions. it is unorthodox but it worked. It's hard work and it's full on, no contact with the outside world but not only will you learn to cope but you will learn to fight back and win, you will never be helpless again."

"What about, Trip, Millie and the others, how do I just tell them I want to disappear for a year."

"You don't! I can take you there now, I will explain to Trip, he will understand."

"I can't just leave..."

"What if it was Millie in here instead of the assistant, what if you blackout like that and get hold of a gun, it's your choice but I think it's best to get you there and get you better as soon as possible." I think about it, and I find myself nodding.

"I can't hurt anyone I love," I whisper, Paul nods and gets up, "Stay here, I will get the security to take Millie home." I put my head in my hands as Paul leaves to sort out the mess I have made. I clench my eyes shut, refusing to stare at the utter devastation I caused to this changing room in the matter of minutes. I don't want to leave, and my heart feels like it's cracking into a million pieces at the thought of leaving the only family I have ever had, but what will I do next time, what if I hurt one of them. I may have survived a lot already, but I won't survive that! I need to do something before I become a monster, before I lose myself completely. Paul's right, I have to leave, I have to get fixed, and I have to go now, I couldn't even handle a few hours out of the house, and it will only get worse.

Chapter Twenty-Three
5 years later

I stare down the scope of the sniper rifle as I lay in the dirt being as still as a statue, two hours I have been here and the sick fuck hasn't stepped foot in his office, I have been tailing this guy for months and this is the first opportunity I have had to take him out and I will not move until the job is done. I think about the stuff in the folder I was sent about him when I was paid to take him out, the deprived shit he has done is unbelievable, well unbelievable to normal people, I am used to reading about the horrible evil people in the world since Paul dropped me off at the Temple. Not in a million years did I Imagine this would be what I would become when I walked through those doors, but I must say he didn't lie, the Temple was the best thing for me then and they saved me, it just so happens that it fucked me too. I watch as Franco Depalio walks across his big office and sits in his comfy desk chair, I smirk even though no one can see it, I take in a large breath and as I release it, I pull the trigger. The bullet soars through the air and I watch through the scope as it sinks into Franco's brain via his left temple, he slumps forward Immediately. Another job to tick off my list, no more will he harm innocent children to make money, that fact alone washes away any guilt I should have. I quickly grab my shit and dart for my car, I throw everything into the boot and jump into the driver's seat, dirt flies around as I turn the car and speed off. I dial the number for the Temple and listen through loudspeakers as the receptionist answers the phone

"Hello and welcome to the database of Human resources, do you have an extension?"

"58774." I say,

"Ahh good afternoon Ruby Reaper how may I assist you today?"

"Job 3782 is complete, please send payment."

"Very good, Miss Reaper, we will send payment in due course and we will be in touch if we have any other HR issues that need your expertise." I hang up the phone and drop it into my lap. After two hours of driving my Lambo at top speed I finally pull into my garage and grab my shit out of the boot of the car and take it all into my home. I walk through the hallway into the main living area, I go to the fireplace and place my hand underneath, I hear the familiar click of the lock I grab the edge of the fire place and pull it open I duck as I enter the secret staircase which leads to a metal door, I put my hand on the scanner and it quickly opens. I walk into the room and make quick work of putting my guns away in their rightful place along with all the other weapons I have down here. I take a seat at my desk and turn on my computer it's three screens coming to life. I do what I normally do after finishing a job and it's so soothing to have this little routine. I take everything I have on the dearly departed and secure it into a protected file and put it into the hard drive. I then check to see what jobs I have outstanding and if I have any leads and after hours of research, I finally check my bank, without fail the Seven Hundred Thousand Euros has been transferred into my offshore account. I turn everything off and secure the door before heading back upstairs to turn into the most boring person ever. While sitting on the couch and watching family guy my phone rings, I glance at the screen and my brows pinch together. What does he want he hardly ever contacts me anymore; I answer the phone and wait for him to speak.

"Skye, I need you again." Paul says and I sigh,

"I thought we said I wouldn't be helping you guys out anymore!" I grumble back,

"I know, I know but we have a problem and right now, I think you are the only one who can help me."

"Fine but you don't tell anyone who I am!"

"I know the rules, Skye. I won't tell anyone as far as they are concerned you are the random assassin that gets shit done."

"Usual spot, Three hours."

"I'll be there." I hang up and flop back onto the sofa facing the ceiling. I knew he would call again; I need to stay away from them, it's only going to get me caught by trip and I don't need that, I don't want him to see what I have become, and I really don't want Millie to see it. They probably hate me for leaving like I did and never coming back, I have not spoken to any of them since I left, except Paul that is. What would I even say to them if they caught me around, I shake my head and get dressed. As I pull on my leather trousers, black crop top and leather jacket I think about how my life would have been if fucking Jay never got to me, I would have been with the love of my life, my best friend and the family who loved me, instead I have become a monster, fair enough I am the monster who other monsters have nightmares about but still, I have lost my innocence, dirtied my soul and I live a lonely life filled with death. I always think what if I never went to the Temple, but that would have been so much worse, my mental state was awful, and I don't know what I would have done but I don't think I would have survived. I stare at myself in the mirror and take in how different I look, I now have a long bob that is a platinum blonde colour and it's dead straight, my make up is minimal except from the winged liner that sweeps my eyelids, I have much more muscle tone all over my body from the vigorous training I do daily to keep my body ready for anything and then there's the darkness in my eyes that comes from deep within my soul, that is the biggest change in my appearance and anyone who knew me before will know how much evil I have done since I left just by looking into my eyes. I sigh and head out to the garage, I check the pistol is still in the seat of my Ducati Monster and then pull the helmet over my head. I swing my leg over and once I am on the road; I push this machine as fast as it will go and enjoy the wind whipping past me as I go to visit the past.

I pull up in the abandoned warehouse opposite the black SUV, as I get off the bike the driver door opens, I spin around and take my helmet off placing it on the bike as I turn to face Paul, a smile on my face to see someone I care about after so long. My face falls as I stare into Trip's eyes, the many emotions flitting through them until he lands on anger.

"This is a joke, right?" He spits, I lift my chin and take two steps toward him,

"No, Paul called me to do a job, so here I am." Trip scoffs and I narrow my eyes at him.

"Oh, so you're telling me that your Ruby Reaper the so-called nightmare of monsters, yeah right. What kind of game are you playing?"

"Believe what you want Trip, either you have a job for me or you don't, I don't exactly need the pay day so I am happy to go right back fucking home." He takes a step towards me until we are inches away from each other.

"Tell me, why didn't you come home, why choose this over your family."

"Don't Trip, you won't like the answer."

"I think I can figure it out on my own, you really are fucked up aren't you. Well, if it makes you happy, here. Go rip another part of your soul away." He pushes the folder into my chest and I take it. I try to ignore his words but I know they will eat at me once I get out of here. I scan the first few pages of the folder and chuckle,

"Really, you the all mighty Trip can't take out this guy! I will have it done in two days, be here same time to transfer my cash!" I turn to leave but his hand curls around my arm and he spins me back to face him. He runs his fingers down my cheek and I have to stop myself from leaning into his touch, the usual sparks fly through my veins and I hate the power he obviously still holds over me.

"Meet me at the house when it's done, with proof, you have explaining to do." With that he storms back to the car and I get out of there as quickly as I can.

I contemplate going back home but the job Trip wants me to do is on the way and I know exactly where this guy will be in an hour, I have been trailing him for months, as the Temple want him taken out too, two birds and one stone. I am fucking pissed right now which makes the decision to go end some scumbag right the fuck now so much easier, what was Paul thinking? Why would he send Trip of all people to meet me, I kick up the speed on my bike and make my mind go blank as I head to my second victim of the day.

I walk into the seedy motel that Vince Manning is currently using to stick his dick into a hooker, I walk up the stairs and my foot steps are silent, I get to the third floor and peek through the door to the hallway and as expected I spot his single bodyguard pacing up and down in front of the room Vince is in. I walk through the door and pretend I am looking for my room number as I look at every door I walk past, I get to the goon guarding the door and he doesn't even give me a second look, he doesn't deem me as a threat, oh how wrong he is. When I have walked past him, and his back is to me I spin and grab his head twisting it fast and hard. The body falls to the floor, his life gone before he even knew it, I open the door and creep into the room shutting the door behind me, I instantly get a view I never wanted to see Vince's fat arse is out as he bangs the hooker who looks like she's going to be sick. The hooker notices me and I put my finger to my mouth telling her to be quiet, I grab the gun from the back of my leather trousers and point it to Vince's head, he turns to me when he feels the cold metal of the silencer on his temple his eyes wide as he stares at me.

"Get out." I say to the hooker, and she nods vigorously as she scrambles off the bed. "Oh, and you didn't see a thing, I can come after you too if you did." The poor girl looks terrified as she runs out of the room still naked.

"What do you want?" Vince asks his voice a little shaky for someone who kidnaps women to sell them as slaves. This guy is one of the worst, he will do anything to make money, I just wonder how he is causing problems for Trip, Trip is a bad guy yes but not fucking evil like this mother fucker.

"I don't want anything, I just got a call and when Ruby Reaper gets a call, she always gets the job done." At the mention of my alias his eyes go even wider and I pull the trigger and just like that another job ticked off the list, one job done two paydays, I smirk at that thought then my eyebrows pinch together as I remember Trip wants proof. For fuck's sake I am the best assassin this side of the world and that bastard has the cheek to ask me to waste my time with proof, I look around and don't spot anything I can use, Fuck me! I grab the guy's suit trousers and find his wallet and phone in his pocket so I pop them in mine. I groan as I get my switch blade out and hack at the guy's finger. By the time I am finished my hands are covered in blood and I have a very poorly cut finger in my hand I grab a pillow off the bed and use the case to pop the finger in and wrap it around so I can carry it out of here. I go into the bathroom and scrub the blood off me, when I look decent enough to be a part of civilisation again, I get the fuck out.

Chapter Twenty-Four

I roll up to the gate on my Ducati the next evening, I pull up my visor to speak to the security, surprisingly I am still on the list, according to the guards I was never taken off. I race down the huge driveway and park my bike up and enter the estate through the front door, I stalk towards Trip's office and I am shocked that I haven't seen anyone yet. I walk into Trip's office and shut the door behind me, Trip stares at me and then abruptly ends his phone call without a word. I walk to his desk and place the finger wallet and phone in front of him before I sit down in front of him. Trip looks from me to the items and back to me a few times s, when I raise an eyebrow, he clears his throat.

"I take it this is my proof?"
"Yup."
"Ok, I'll have your money transferred within the hour." I nod, get up and head towards the door, just as I put my hand on the doorknob Trip speaks and it stops me dead in my tracks,
"Skye, please, tell me why." I shake my head still staring at the door. I try not to flinch as his hands slam against the door either side of my head and I shiver when I feel his breath on my neck. "Was it something I did?" His voice is low but I can hear the pain in his tone and I look down at my hand still wrapped around the doorknob.

"Trip, I can't do this, please!" I whisper, his hand trails down my arm and he grabs my wrist, turning me to face him. He pulls me into him and wraps his arms around me so tight it is like he is hanging on for dear life.

"I still love you, Skye. I don't know why, but I can't just let you go." I slam my hands against his chest, anger seeping out of me, he stumbles back a step and I stare him down with a glare that could kill.

"You don't love me! How can you when your happily married now, what would she think about your little confession!" I spit and I watch as confusion spreads across his face.

"What are you talking about."

"Really, I saw you Trip! Don't act dumb."

"Skye, I have no idea what you're on about."

"Ok, let me paint the picture for you. Six months after I left, I got to come back for 48 hours to see my family, but when I got back here all I saw was magazines with you and some brown hair bitch on the cover announcing your engagement. I thought no, that can't be true and came here. I was walking along the road to come in when I saw you leave the house hand in hand with her and you kissed her before getting in the car. So, I turned around and never looked back, so you hate me because I didn't come back, I hate you because you made it so I couldn't."

"Skye, it wasn't like that"

"Fuck this! I don't need your bullshit excuses, I am out!" I turn back around, and swing open the door so hard it bangs against the wall. I storm through the house and leave as quickly as I can, not looking back. I get on my bike and race down the driveway and through the gates, I am about to turn off Trip's

Street when two blacked out cars drive past me, I see into the windscreen of the second one and I know the passenger. Who is that? Shit! That was Vince's second in command, I watch in my mirrors as they crash into the gate of Trip's house and speed down the driveway. Fuck! It is not my problem, this is not my problem, oh fuck it, this is so my problem now. I groan as I spin the bike around and race after the car. I watch as they all pile out and race into the house with their guns out. I jump off the bike as quickly as I can and run after them, I can hear the wailing of the alarm going off inside the house. I hope to god everyone got inside the panic room in time. I spot the security edging closer towards the house but they are too slow, they are scanning everything. I burst into the foyer and walk with my chin up towards the two goons standing keeping watch.

"Hi boys!" I say with a smirk, "I assume your friends are ransacking the house looking for Trip?"

"Who the fuck are you?"

"I am your worst nightmare." They both run at me and I fight with little effort a few punches and kicks and they are both on the ground. I pull my switch knife out and slit both of their throats. I see a walkie talkie on one of the guys and I grab it.

"Hey dickheads, I've killed your friends, come here and face me or I will hunt every last one of you down." Footsteps pound along the hallways and down the stairs until seven big ass men and Vince's second are all standing in front of me looking very pissed at the sight of little old me standing over their two dead friends. Vince's nods his head to his men and they rush at me, the closest to me raises his gun I grab his wrist and pull him to me so his shot goes over my shoulder and I ram my knife in his gut and pull up so his insides are out of his body as he drops to the floor, I spin around and kick the next guy so hard he ends on the floor. I throw my knife and it lands in one of the guys eyes killing him on Impact, while one was watching the knife hurtle through the air, I grab him from behind and use his body to protect mine as I squeeze his finger on his trigger and kill three more of the guys before is twist his arm and make him shoot himself in the head. Blood and brains splatter all over me, I smirk at the next lackey who comes at me and he stumbles in fear, I know I look completely psycho at this point. He takes a shot but I doge out of the way, sliding across the floor to the guy with my knife in his eye, I yank it out and throw it again, it goes straight into the dickheads thigh and he grunts in pain as he buckles, I walk over and snap his neck, as I walk over one of the body's I bend down to grab his gun from the floor, I walk until I am face to face with Vince's second and he raises his gun so it's and inch from my forehead.

"Who the fuck are you?" He growls, and I smile sweetly.

"Me, I am no one." I watch his jaw clench and then his eyes dart to his gun, the movement is so quick that most people would miss it, but that's my queue to move. I spin as he presses the trigger in the next instant, I am at his side with my gun pressed to his temple as the gun in his hand, blood spilling down my arm where the bullet grazed my shoulder. "Say hi to Vince for me." I pull the trigger and he drops to the floor. I take a deep breath as I drop the gun to the floor beside him, I look around and finally take note of the pure carnage. There are Ten dead bodies, internal body parts, brains and a shit ton of blood covering the marble floor. I pace up and down the foyer as I start panicking, they are all going to see exactly how much of a monster I have become. If I remember rightly the panic room won't reopen for another forty minutes or so, I could just leave, and I won't have to see the disappointment and hate on their faces. They are probably watching me on the cameras now, I look up to the corner of the room and spot the tiny camera. I shake my head and go for the door; I need to get out of here! My phone buzzes in my pocket as I reach the door, I pull it out and see Paul's name flashing on the screen, I hesitate but eventually answer.

"Skye!" Millie's voice registers in my head and a tear falls from my eye.

"I am sorry, Millie." I go to hang up,

"Wait! You have nothing to be sorry for! You get your arse back in this house right now!" I take a few steps back and look back to the camera. "Good, now you are not running from me again, you will be here when I get out of this stupid room."

"Millie, please, I can't be here." I sigh, knowing She's already won.

"This is your home, and I miss my best friend. Go to my old room and get cleaned up, if you leave, I will hunt you down and drag you back by your hair."

"Fine, I'll stay for a bit, but once you're out I will be going."

"Yeah, we will see." The phone goes dead, and I stomp to the stairs, I take two at a time and push open Millie's door when I get to it. The rooms bare, wait she said old room, a pang of pain hit my heart as I look around, it looks exactly as it did when I woke up here the day Trip saved me. I shake off the feelings trying to come up, I don't need them right now, I go straight to the bathroom, stripping my clothes off and I get into the shower. I stand there for a moment and let the heat soak into my skin before I scrub my whole body from head to toe, after fifteen minutes the water finally runs clear, and I get out wrapping a towel around me. I look in the mirror and shudder as I realise, I also washed my makeup off and now the jagged scar that covers half my face is on show. I scramble through the draws looking for something, anything to cover it but there is nothing.

"Fuck!" I walk out of the bathroom and sit on the edge of the bed with my head in my hands. They know about the scar, they won't care! I try and convince myself, but I know it's not them it's me, I hate this fucking scar and I hate that it affects me so much, I just don't want anyone to see it. I don't know how long I just sit there repeating the same thoughts in my head but I am jolted out of it when the bedroom door slams and locks, I look up to see Trip standing there, then I hear Millie banging on the door.

"If you upset her Trip, I will come for you!" She continues to bang and then she stops "Fine but I want to see her straight after you!" I hear her stomp away and I try not to smile.

"What do you want?" He doesn't move from the door but I see his brows pinch as his gaze focuses on my hand covering my scar.

"I want to say thank you, for what you did today." I look away from him and shrug.

"I wasn't going to just leave you to deal with them, what if they got to Rina or Millie." I whisper, Trip pushes off the door and comes Infront of me he kneels, so his face is the same level as mine. He takes the hand that's on the cheek and pulls it away gently, he looks at the scar, but his eyes don't show disgust like I expect, they soften and then he looks me in my eyes.

"You don't ever have to hide your scars, especially not from me. You are the most beautiful woman I have ever seen, inside and out."

"Where's your wife?" I ask, Trip runs his hand down his face and stands up, his hand reaching out,

"I need to show you something." I stand up and he looks hurt when he lowers his hand, he leads me out of the bedroom and Dow the hall until we get to his room. I follow him in and look around quickly noticing all the girly touches in the room, it hurts to see it even though I expected it. "That girl you saw me with, the whole thing was fake." My eyes snap to his, "I needed to get her dad to sign a business deal and she needed to get him off her back about getting married, she just wanted to run away with her girlfriend and so we pretended we were engaged, he signed the deal and a month later we broke up, he thinks she is so heartbroken that he hasn't bothered her about marrying since, she finally lives her own life." I stand there staring at him for a moment before looking around the room again, taking more notice of the girl's stuff and then it hits me.

"This is all my stuff! You never got rid of it. "I whisper, Trip takes slow steps towards me as he stares me down and with each step, he takes I take one back.

"I never gave up. I always knew you would come home." I hit the wall and he traps me in his big arms on either side of my head. "I never stopped loving you." I stare into his deep green eyes and stares into mine, I can see every emotion in him and I can feel that he is telling me the honest truth and I feel my resolve snap inside of me. I reach up and run my hand in his hair, when I reach the back of his neck, I pull him down closer to me, I go on my tip toes and I smile when my lips brush his. The kiss is deep and messy, lips teeth and tongues crash together. I pull back panting and I grab his shirt in both hands and pull, buttons fly everywhere and Trip raises an eyebrow when I smirk. I run my hands down his skin as I slide the remains of shirt off. His hands land on my waist and he picks me up, the towel falls to the floor in a heap, he turns and carry's me to the bed and I lean my face down to his to kiss him. We don't break apart even when he places me on the bed, I run my hands down the hard muscles of his chest and he shudders above me, I unbutton his jeans and use my feet to push them and his boxers down.

"Fuck, I can't wait any more, I need you now." He's panting as the words rush out of his mouth and I nod, knowing exactly what he means. I am ready for him and I am covered for protection. He lines himself up with me and slowly fills me with every long hard inch of him, trip groans and leans down to take my mouth with his, he starts to speed up and his thrusts become harder and I feel trip smirk as he swallows my moans. His hand roams down my body heating my skin where he touches, his fingers slide between us and he rubs my clit in the perfect way making me arch my back as the pleasure builds in me. I dig my nails into his back and he groans, the sound tips me over the edge and I tremble under him as I ride out the orgasm. When I have got over the aftershocks, I plant my foot on the bed and flip us so quickly that I chuckle at the shock on Trip's face, I am a lot stronger now and it shows. I sink down on him and he feels Impossibly deeper now, his hands land on my hips and his grip is going to leave fingerprint bruises on my skin. My second orgasm starts to build quickly when Trip thrusts up to meet my movements and within minutes I am crying out as it hits, Trip jerks under me as he grunts my name with his release and I lay on his chest trying to catch my breath. After a while oh of our breathing returns to normal and I roll off of him and the bed and head to the bathroom. I use the toilet and clean myself up before going into the walk-in wardrobe and finding a new outfit. I cringe when I think of how downstairs must look covered in blood that I spilt.

"You're not going, are you?" I spin around to look at him and the broken look on his face crushes me.

"Trip, I am going to have to go at some point and soon, I have a job and a house and..."

"You are an assassin, you can do that from here, and sell the house. Just come home."

"I... I would put you all in danger, look what happened here tonight, all because of me." I look to the floor ashamed of what they all saw. "I am not the girl you loved; I am a monster now." Trip comes over to me and wraps me up in his big arms and crushes me against him.

"You are not a monster; you are more like a vengeful angel who hurts the bad to save the innocent. Everyone in our circles knows about you and the real monsters are the ones you go after. You loved me even after you saw and heard of the bad shit I do, I can accept you for who you are now and I still love you anyway, if not more. You protected us even though you didn't need to or have to, we are the bad guys not you. And what happened was not your fault, they didn't come here because you killed that scum bag, they came here because I made sure they knew I was behind it. It was my fault."

"But, Millie, Rina, the boys they must hate me. How can I stay if there's even a chance of them getting hurt."

"I put them all in danger every day and I make sure they stay as safe as possible and you will do the same, they don't hate you, they never could they love you and they miss you. Just talk to them, you'll see."

"Ok, I will talk to them but I make no promises." Trip nods and kisses my forehead then he turns to grab some clothes and I finish getting dressed, I take a deep breath to steel my nerves as I am about to face the family, I abandoned to become a killer.

Chapter Twenty-Five

"Millie?" I tap on Tiao's door as Trip said she moved in here, no answer I go down the stairs and I am shocked to see most of the carnage from earlier has been cleaned up, some of the security are just finishing up. I pop my had in the living room and it's empty so I head into the kitchen where I walk in on everyone. They are all talking and they all look really serious, that is until Rina looks up and her eyes lock onto mine.

"Gracie al field, la mi ragazza e tornata a casa " She waves her hands as she basically runs at me and pulls me into her arms. When she finally lets me go, I look at the others who have all gotten off their chairs. They all look at Millie and wait for her response.

"You have some explaining to do!" She looks furious and I am holding my breath. "You have to tell me everything, how did you do all that earlier? Where have you been? Why did you not call me!" She comes over and wraps me in a hug a huge smile on her face.

"You're not mad?" She shrugs,

"Bitch, you were traumatised I can forgive that, but try it again and I will hunt you down and drag you home." Tiao and Luca push Millie out of the way as they come in for their hug.

"Thank god your back, Millie has been insufferable." Luca whispers in my ear and I smile, Tiao hears him and pushes him and they both give me some space as they start play fighting. Paul is next and he comes over and gives me a man hug slapping me on the back, I raise an eyebrow but he just shrugs.

"I am glad your back."

"See I told you." Trip says from behind me.

"Told her what?" Tiao asks,

"Skye has it in her head that we think she's a monster now and it's best if she goes again." They all look at me with fierce glares.

"Do not even think about it, you are not going away again." Millie says

"But..."

"No buts, if you leave then I come with you." Millie states

"And if Millie goes then I have to go with her." Tiao says grabbing her hand.

"And if Tiao goes, I am coming and so is Rina " Luca adds

"If they go, I go " Paul shrugs and I look to Trip who's grinning like the Cheshire fucking cat.

"Is your house big enough for all of us?" He says and I sigh.

"I fucking missed you bunch of insufferable, arrogant arseholes!" They all come at me, I am in the middle of a group hug, and everyone starts laughing including me.

※

I SPEND THE NIGHT CATCHING everyone up on the last five years of my life and they catch me up on theirs, things haven't changed much around here and it feels like home again, I thought there would be an adjustment period but it's like how it was before I went to Paris and I swear I haven't felt so content since. We all got a few hours' sleep and now we are all getting into the cars to pack up my shit and move it back home, they wouldn't even give it a few days, they want to know I am back and I am back to stay.

"So, what am I expecting when we get to this house of yours?" Millie asks as she drives us out of the driveway, the others took a car each and I will be driving my own back.

"Not a lot, it's a nice small house with basic furniture."

"So, no secret lair with guns and stuff?"

"Are you basing this off of Mr and Mrs smith?"

"Is that film wrong? So, you don't have a secret room with all your weapons and shit?" I smirk and she screams,

"Omg, I knew it, you are so badass now." I chuckle and shake my head.

"So, you and Tiao, still serious?" I ask and she smiles,

"Yeah, he makes me really happy. What about you and Trip, things seem as hot as ever between you." She wiggles her eyebrows and I roll my eyes.

"Yeah, so far so good but I have literally been back for less than 24 hours so who knows."

"He never stopped looking for you, that guy will never let you go unless you really want to leave."

"I don't know, I am not the same person anymore, you saw what I did to those pricks yesterday, I am a stone-cold killer now." I sigh and then glare at Millie when she full on laughs.

"I am sorry but if anything, you fit in with his life even more now, you tell me a better match than a mafia boss and a trained assassin? And you didn't see his face when he watched you do your stuff on those feeds from the panic room, he was like a dog on heat. They do some fucked up shit on a daily basis, they try and hide it from me the best they can but I know what they're doing and honestly, I couldn't care less, same as I don't care that my best friend kills people for her career. All I care about is family and our family is finally whole again." I just stare out the window going over her words, I mean she does have a point they kill people and do a lot of shady shit and now so do I, I could be an asset to them if they let me. All of a sudden, my whole future looks a lot brighter.

"Your right! Maybe just maybe this can all work out for the better."

We soon pull up outside my little house and we get out of the car the boys park on the road as I only have enough space in my driveway for one. We all walk in as I unlock the doors and everyone takes a good look around.

"What do you want to take and what do you want to leave?" Millie asks.

"I just want my clothes and that from upstairs, Millie can you pack up everything in there while me and the boys pack up the, you know what?" I smirk at her and she stomps her foot.

"I have no problem doing that but I want to see it and I want to see it now."

"See what?" Luca asks, I smile and head to the fireplace as they all follow, Millie up front and centre. I reach under the mantle and pull the leaver which unlocks the door.

"Ready? "I smile as Millie nods her head and bounces from one foot to another. I grab the edge of the fire place and pull it open; I duck in and go down the stairs everyone follows quickly, I put my hand on the scanner and the metal door opens and Millie gasps as she pushes past me to get into the room first, the boys follow and I watch from just inside the door as they take it all in.

"Holy shit." Trip says at the same time Luca whistles.

"Is there a war we should know about?" Tiao teases as he runs his fingers over some of my weapons.

"Where the fuck are we going to put it all?" Paul asks and I shrug

"You're going to need a room like this at the house, how did you even do it?" Trip asks

"I have a few contacts, one of these can be built in a week if you know the right people, if there's already a secret room like this house had, a few hours to get the security and systems set up."

"Right, lets figure that out later, let's just get all of this back to the house."

"I'll get started on your clothes and stuff, I assume you don't want any furniture or house bits?" Millie asks and I shake my head, she heads back up the stairs to help as much as she can. I pull out my phone and dial The Temple.

"Hello and welcome to the database of Human Resources, do you have an extension?" The receptionist asks as usual,

"58774." I reply,

"Good morning, Ruby, Reaper. How may I assist you today?"

"I need to go off grid for a week or two, also I will be relocating during this time so expect the server to be down for a few days also, I will need to get new security measures in place before I can have it back online." I l turn around to see all the guys and they look at me like I've grown a second head.

"Perfect, can I assist with anything else?" She says cheerily,

"Actually, could you find out who installed my last security set up and get them to give me a call later today?"

"Sure thing, have a good break." I hang up the phone.

"What?" I ask as the guys are still staring,

"You are like a real life 007!" Tiao says and I snort a laugh,

"Not quite." I reply,

"What's the server all about?" Paul asks

"It's one of the eight servers that the Temple have, it holds details of all sorts of shit that can help the guys do their jobs. I am trusted to keep it safe."

"So, your high up in the ranks then?" Paul asks and I shrug.

"They don't own me; I am my own boss but they trust me so yeah you could say that."

"Right, let's get this packed up, Luca you can tackle the computer, I will warn you the wiring is a mess behind there, there are cases on top of all the units for the guns get as many as you can in them." I go to the first gun display and reach on my tip toes for the case on top, Trip comes behind me and presses his body to mine as he grabs the case, before stepping back he whispers in my ear.

"I am not going to lie, but seeing you like this, with all these guns and being a total boss is hot as fuck." Heat pools between my thighs and I struggle to stay focused on the task ahead. I grab the rifle and throw it to Trip who catches it effortlessly. We get around the room and pack up the guns quite quickly. It takes a few hours but eventually the room is packed up and ready to be loaded into the cars. Tiao is still staring at the box with the grenades in and I chuckle at him.

"Dude, they are not toys."

"I know but I really want to play with them." Luca punches him in the arm and I laugh, Tiao, Paul and Luca start hauling the cases upstairs and I turn to Trip.

"Is that it for this room?" Trip asks and I walk over to the back of the room and push the wall to open the secret cabinet.

"Just this left." I pull out two large wheels and pull them behind me as I go to the door where Trip is waiting,

"What's in these ones?" He asks

"Two Million in cash and some fake passports." I say as I pass him to take them upstairs.

"Why do you need Two mil in cash?"

"I'll show you later, don't tell the others just yet. "I walk through the house and into the garage and pop the boot to the Lambo I put the cases in along with some of my riding gear from around the garage and close it, Trip leans against the door frame and I step into him, he automatically puts his arms around me and I melt into his hold.

"Trip, I am so sorry." I say, my voice breaking a bit.

"Sorry for what?"

"For leaving like I did, for not coming back, for everything. I was so selfish for doing that to you and it hurt like hell to leave you but I need you to know how sorry I am." His hold on me grows tighter and I close my eyes needing to have this moment with him.

"You don't have anything to be sorry about, you did what you needed to and I will always stand by you, no matter what, do I hate that I have missed you every day for five years. Yes! Do I hate that you were going through all of that shit! Yes. Do I hate that you were alone in this house for years. Yes! But now your back and as long as you'll have me, I am here for you, you have nothing to be sorry for." He states as if it's fact and I raise my head to look into his eyes, he leans down and kisses me so softly, so full of love and tenderness that I have no choice but to believe his words whole heartedly.

<hr>

AS SOON AS WE GET HOME Trip orders his men to unload all of the cars and put the stuff in the basement, He is not happy with any of his men and he has asked me to help retrain them along with Paul and Luca. I did wonder why they were all so slow to get to the house and then they didn't even come in to help me when the house was being attacked by Vincent's guys. So instead of overhauling his goons we are going to weed out the weak and retrain the ones who should know better, according to Paul they have all got a bit lazy as not much happens at the house, which is true. Trip leads me down to the basement and I instantly recognise one of the rooms to be the one I was chained up in once upon a time, we pass that door and go to the last door down the creepy corridor and he opens it showing me a huge room that's completely empty.

"Can you convert this into your headquarters?" I bash him with my elbow and he laughs.

"It should do nicely, I will need to decorate and get the security systems set up and some new furniture but yeah, thank you."

"You're welcome." He smiles and grabs my hand as he leads me back into the hallway, his men have just started to fill the hall with my stuff and Trip gestures to the room and they move quickly to please him. I continue up the stairs and wonder into the living room and just stop and stare into it, it's weird being back here, it's fucking insane that it feels like I never left. How can this house, the people in this home bring me so much peace, so much security and how did I not realise this is where I should have been? I will never regret going to the temple as I needed that to sort my head out, but not coming back when I was finished there may be the biggest mistake of my life.

"Hey." I jump as Paul comes to stand beside me,

"Don't sneak up on people!" I admonish and he just gives a slight chuckle.

"You were lost in your own world there, are you ok?" He asks and I shrug a shoulder,

"Better than I have been in years, but I, I just feel so guilty for leaving, for not coming back. Trip has literally left his room the same as the day I left, to see all my stuff every day must have been torture and Millie, I abandoned her after dragging her here in the first place. Never mind the rest of you who welcomed me into this family and made me feel like I belonged, like I was actually part of a family who would do anything for me and I just left. what kind of person does that make me?"

"It makes you human, look the main thing is that your back, your healthy and you're not tormented by PTSD and trauma anymore and we all just wanted what was best for you. You did the right thing, no one in this house thinks any different, Trip wasn't tormented by you being gone, he knew where I took you, he didn't move your stuff because he wanted you to come back and feel at home. Millie has excelled in her career and she and Tiao's relationship went from strength to strength, she missed you every day, we all did but she knew you would be back and that's why she said no when Tiao proposed, she was furious that he would dare do that without you there." My eyes go wide, and then so do Paul's, I storm out of the room and up the stairs,

"Millie!" I shout, she comes out of her room just as I get to it and I put my hands on my hips,

"What's wrong with you?" She asks and I scoff.

"You are a dumb cow sometimes!"

"What did I do?"

"You paused your own happiness just because I was so fucked up, I couldn't be here, why the fuck would you say no to him?" I am nearly screaming at her; I am so angry with her and I feel so guilty that I affected this too.

"I wasn't ready to rush into a future without you! I just didn't want to admit that you might not come back and I needed you to be there when all the good was happening!" A tear falls from Millie's eye and runs down her cheek. I sigh and pull her in for a hug.

"I am so sorry, Millie. I am a selfish bitch and I hate that we were apart for so long."

"It's ok, now we can all just get on with life and leave all the shit behind." We stand there hugging each other for a good five minutes before she pulls away, she smiles a bit when she looks over my shoulder, I look too and see all the guys standing there watching us.

"I am sorry to you guys too; I should have just come home."

"We don't forgive you." Luca states and I nod my head looking to the floor," Because there is nothing to forgive. Your family, and you needed time, who are we to say you can't have it." He continues and I snap my head up to look at him,

"We know your sorry and we wish you weren't, you have been forced to live a life someone else controlled and now we know for sure that you want to be here, no one's forcing you, you're not her out of fear, guilt or because Trip saved you." Tiao adds,

"I sent you to the Temple because that's what you needed, you made the choice and we supported that, we don't know why you didn't come back after you left there and we don't care why, you needed to figure things out on your own." Paul smiles,

"Paul knew you were about the whole time and we knew Paul knew so we could have found you if we wanted but it wasn't our choice to make, you had to find your own way back to us and you did, I mean Paul gave you the nudge but you could have gone anytime but instead you willingly got your stuff and came home. We couldn't ask for more than that, even if it took you twenty years, we would have all been here and fucking happy to see you. No matter what happens we are a family and that doesn't ever stop." Trip says, I look to the ceiling trying and failing to stop the waterfall of tears, I chuckle and look at them all.

"Your all sappy arseholes, but I love you all anyway." I smile as they all wrap their arms around me in a giant group hug. When they finally release me and Millie Trip takes my hand.

"No more worrying about the past, let's just continue from here."

"Agreed." Luca and Tiao state as Millie and Paul nod their heads.

"Ok, but we need to deal with one more thing from the past, before we can move on and never look back."

Chapter Twenty-Six

"Skye?" Trip pokes his head out the door of the closet as I sit in the bed with a coffee, it's been a week since we all got our feelings out and I can say that I no longer feel sad or guilty, I am just happy to be around them all again and my life finally seems right.

"Yeah." I reply,

"Erm, these cases, are they just staying in the doorway of our closet?"

"I am not sure what to do with them, they're not exactly for me."

"What do you mean, not exactly yours?" I put the coffee on the bedside table and go to the walk-in wardrobe, I slip past Trip and grab both cases wheeling them to the bed and placing them on top of it. Trip comes to stand next to me as I use my fingerprint to undo the padlocks.

"Take a look." I wave towards the cases before sitting back on the bed. Trip opens each case and picks up one of the many passports, his eyes go wide as he opens one.

"The fuck?" He then grabs another looking inside and another and another. "What is this?"

"It's my last resort, my back up, my get out of jail free card."

"But you're the only one without a passport, these are all ours?" I shrug.

"What's going on, why were you worried about us even though you had nothing to do with us for so long?" A pang of guilt slices through me, maybe I am not so guilt free as I thought.

"Just because I stayed away didn't mean I stopped caring about any of you. And there is one person that I need to locate and deal with but can't. Those suitcases were for if he ever showed up here, or the slim chance someone found out my identity and came after you guys."

"We don't need these, Skye we can handle anything that comes to our door, as long as we do it together." I nod my head and stare at the cases, "What do I do with it?"

"The money, fucking spend it, invest, whatever. The passports we will put in the safe in case we ever need them, ok?"

"Ok," I smile feeling a lot better about the passports still being around, if we ever need to get out, we will need those, everyone in this house has enough money so we are all good on that.

"What about Jay, we have looked for him too but nothing."

"He's gone deep underground, there's one thing that would bring him out of hiding,"

"You."

"Yeah, me. As much as I am over everything that happened, I am still too weak to be bait for that monster. I have this fear that I will still freeze when face to face with him." Archer kneels before me and takes my hands in his,

"You are not weak, even if you did freeze that does not define you. I cannot promise you that we will always be there, there are no amount of precautions we could take to make sure you were never alone, but I doubt you want that. I know that if he came for you, you will not freeze, you will end him and if I am there, I will make sure he dies at your hand. You will defeat your monster baby." A small smile plays at my lips,

"I love that you would rather support me doing it than be my knight in shining armour, it's so twenty-first century of you."

"Are you making fun of me?" He says with a grin, I shrug my shoulders. "You are in for it now!" He says as he pounces, I end up wriggling on the bed, him on top of me as he tickles me so hard, I can't breathe.

"St stop, I I am so sorry," I stutter through the laughter, Trip stops torturing me and lays beside me, he threads his fingers in mine and I wonder how a gesture so small can be so fucking perfect.

⁓⁂⁓

"YOU NEED TO GET FROM your stations to the house in one and a half minutes, you all are stationed in the inner ring of the house so there is no excuse. We will stay here all day and all night until every single one of you touches the wall in under ninety seconds." I shout to the line of guards,

"Your jobs are officially on the line, so you need to impress us and fast." I hear Paul say as start jogging back to the house. I lean against the wall and get out the stopwatch, "And go!" I hear over the walkie talkie and set the stopwatch off. It hits one minute thirty and not even half have made it.

"You lot that are touching the wall, go grab a seat and a beer, we might be here a while." They go off with smiles and I roll my eyes, "Paul, I am sending the ones that didn't make it back I'll time them, they're not having a break until I say so." I say down the walkie talkie.

"That suits me just fine." He replies. It takes another minute or two but finally all the guards get to me, most out of breath and sweating profusely.

"That was awful, start running back, you have ninety seconds from now." They all groan but do as they are told and start running again. I shake my head as I watch them run at a snail's pace,

"That bad?" Trip asks,

"Did you even do fitness checks when you hired these goons?" I ask as he wraps his arms around me pulling my back into his front.

"I used to, but not so much anymore, there hasn't been an incident in so long we all got lazy and just didn't think about it."

"This is your fault too then, but don't worry, I'll bring them up to scratch."

"I am sure you will." I turn my head to look up at him, but only catch a glimpse before he kisses me intensely. I whip my head round when the stopwatch goes off and I radio Paul,

"Times up, how many?"

"None."

"Jesus, this is going to be a long day."

"They don't think it's possible to run it in that time, they don't think you could do it, so why should they." I smirk.

"Set your timer Paul." I wriggle out of Trip's hold, to get ready to run. "You coming?" I raise an eyebrow in challenge to Trip and luckily, he's in his casual outfit today.

"It's on!"

"And GO!" We take off and at first Trip is in the lead but he soon runs out of momentum and that's when I speed up over taking him easily. His eyes go wide as I pass and he fights through so he speeds up again. We are neck and neck as we get closer and closer to Paul but I beat him by a mere second. He grabs me, lifts me into the air, and spins me around.

"And the winner is..." He smiles up at me and I smack his shoulder to let me down.

"Time?" I ask and Paul chuckles as we stand beside him.

"53 seconds."

"You have no excuse not to be able to do it in ninety any more complaining and you will be asked to leave immediately, take a few minutes to drink water and stretch.

"I'll send Tiao out to take Skye's place for a bit, I need to steal her away."

"Ok." Paul says as Trip grabs my hand and walks me back to the house.

WE ARE GREETED BY THE guy in charge of overhauling my new HQ, as the guys keep calling it, when we get to the main part of the house.

"You're done?" I ask and the guy nods,

"You ready for a tour so I can get out of your hair?"

"Unbelievably ready." I am so excited to see what they have done; the plans were insane but I only got to glance over them. The three of us go down to the basement and past the torture room. The corridor seems shorter now and there is no door in sight. The guy hands me a small remote with two buttons on it,

"The one on the right opens, and the one on the left locks. There is also a hand scanner two hidden in a panel to your right just in case you don't have the remote." I nod my head and press the right button; a door size hole appears from the seamless wall and slides back and to the side so we can walk through as soon as we have it closes again and I press the left button to engage the lock.

"Wow." Trip says staring closely at the wall. The door that leads into my HQ is now visible but it's a different door entirely, Its now fully metal and impenetrable.

"As requested, your friends can get this far, but only you and Trip can unlock this door." I nod as I put my hand on the scanner and my eye towards the retina scanner. The sound of the locks disengaging can be heard echoing around the small space, I take the handle and push the door to show a completely different room to the one Trip showed me last week. The back wall has a long desk pushed up against it, the wall above is filled with dozens of flat screen monitors all different sizes. The server and the PC towers are all hidden behind the desk I am assuming. Beside the doorway is a small seating area, a bit like a booth from a diner but much fancier and there is a little kitchenette in the corner two. Both walls to the sides have top to bottom cabinets that are glass. My weapons are neatly displayed in them, "I have taken the liberty to get you some new gadgets, they are behind the guns in the cabinets they all have secret backs, so feel free to have a look later. I have also hooked up the security system for the house to in here and there is a private connection to the other safe room so you can freely communicate."

"Thank you, it's perfect." He smiles and gestures to the paperwork on the island in the middle of the room.

"Everything you need to know is in there, I will leave you too it."

"Thanks man." Trip shakes his hand as he leaves the room. I click the unlock button so he can actually leave though. "Why did you have the communication set up to the panic room?" Trip asks and I smile.

"This panic room can be used by me you and the others, the other panic room can be used by everyone, If we are all closer to this one, we are coming here. Plus the other one has a timer and I hate that, so I will be coming here to scope things out if another incident happens.

"You go to the panic room that's the closest, you don't risk yourself I know you can handle your own, Skye, but I wouldn't survive if you got yourself killed when you could be locked in one of these rooms."

"I am not promising anything."

All the guys have gathered In my new HQ, Millie has joined us too, I think she thinks she's in some bond movie and is loving every second.

"So, you have not seen any trace of him since the attack in Paris?" Paul asks as he stares at the screens, I rub my hands down my face in frustration.

"No, you can see Jay leaving the hotel and the main part of Paris but then he just disappears, no trace of him since not even on the dark web."

"What have you tried? "Luca asks,

"I run his face through facial recognition software every month and it checks all social media, traffic cams, CCTV literally everything all across the globe. Either he's dead or has a different face."

"Or he's really good at hiding " Millie whispers and I send a pointed glare her way, "Sorry, could he be somewhere where there is no CCTV, no internet basically a desert island?"

"It's a possibility, but you remember him, right? It's not his style, especially for this long, he will be out there somewhere living life, high on drugs probably beating his newest girl." I feel the tension roll off of Trip with that last part.

"The only way he will show himself is to lure him out and the only person that can do that, is you." Taio says and I nod,

"I know, and we are going to have to think hard about actually doing it, I need the prick gone, forever."

"No, there has to be another way, one that doesn't use you as bait. You have said it yourself; you are not ready for that."

"Ok, we look for another way for now, but if and when the time comes, I will make myself be ready, I am ready to get on with my life without looking over my shoulder."

"Agreed." Millie states and we all stare at her, "What I don't know enough to have an input anywhere else." We all burst out in laughter and leave any lingering thoughts about Jay in the panic room.

Chapter Twenty – Seven

I walk into the foyer in my full black leathers and my sniper case, "Whoa, I forgot how hot you look in assassin mode." Trip says as he snakes his hands around my waste from the back of me.

"You have seen it twice so not surprising." He rests his chin on his shoulder holding me tighter.

'Do you have to go be Ruby Reaper right now, I suddenly have something to show you in our room." I laugh, drop the case and spin in his arms, lifting my arms to wrap around the back of his neck.

"As fun as that sounds, this guy does not leave his very guarded, very impenetrable house very often, so this is my only shot for a long while."

"I wish I could come see you in action."

"There is no action, it's a simple sniper shot, and you can come if you want to."

"Let me go get changed." He says with a grin before running up the stairs.

"SO, YOU'RE PLANNING to make the sot when he comes back out of the building?" Trip asks as I position myself behind the sniper that's now set on its stand.

"Nope, see that window over there, that's my shot." I say pointing to the window on the building the other side of the road and two floors lower than us.

"Why, him leaving is a much easier shot, plus how do you know he will even show in the window?"

"Ruby Reaper does not have the reputation she does by taking the as shots, plus what you don't know is this building is the only thing in this world that lie man cares about, in fact from his window is the only viewpoint into seeing that prized possession."

"Ok, I'll bite, what's so important to him that he creeps on it from across the road?"

"His secret son, his one and only heir, not even his son knows he is his son."

"You're kidding?" I shake my head before looking down the scope and one minute later there he is, with a wink to Trip I pull the trigger, the bullet speeds through the air, the glass smashes and hits him right in the eye causing blood and brains to splatter everywhere before he slumps forward.

"How's that for a shot?" I say as I start to dismantle my weapon at speed.

"Yeah, ok, fuck the easy shot." Trip's eyes are wide and he keeps looking between me and the guy.

"We should leave now." He nods and we make our way down the fire escape, thankfully its dark and I've already disabled any CCTV that could see us and go back to the car.

After an hour of driving Trip pulls into a drive through and orders us both burgers, fries and shakes before taking us to a huge country park, we both climb the fence and find a place to sit while we eat. It's the middle of the night and its pitch black here apart from the torches on our phones. We don't talk, we just relax as we rarely get the chance to sit in such a beautiful place with silence all around us. When I've finished my food, I lay down and stare at the twinkly stars that look so magical. Trip does the same and intertwines his fingers through mine.

"You know, I used to stare at the stars every night as a kid."

"Yeah?"

"Yeah, being raised to be a mafia boss, isn't all what it seems, but my Dad did tell me once that, the only way someone like us could be happy is to find the other half of their soul, like he did with Mom, and if we wished to the heavens hard enough the universe would make sure they are put in your life. I wished every night for years for the other half of me, my one true love, my happiness. I am so fucking glad I did because he was right, the universe made sure I would get you." A tear rolls down my cheek as I look at him, my heart thumping so loudly I am sure he can hear it. He turns to look at me and smiles so brightly I wouldn't have needed the torches to see it because I would have felt that smile in my soul. He wipes the tear with his finger,

"You are all I need in this world, Skye and I will do anything to keep you." I don't know what to say, there is nothing I can say to all of that, so I show him my feelings for him instead, I move to lean over him as I kiss him and pour my heart into it. Slowly we touch each other, almost lazily, we eventually strip our clothes and he puts me on my back before dragging every inch of his body over mine. We stare into each other's eyes, letting each other see everything that's hiding inside of us, I only break eye contact when he slowly enters me and my eyes shut as I moan. The pace is slow and exquisite, my hands roam over his chest, his back and in his hair while he kisses me so deeply it came straight out of a fairy-tale. My orgasm builds excruciatingly slowly when he whispers, "I love you, Skye." In my ear I finally tip over that edge, my muscles tightening around him, my fingernails digging into his skin and my legs trembling, he follows me quickly going stiff above me as he calls my name and then he leans forward not putting his weight on my but keeping me in his hold. I stare up at the stars once again over his shoulder and smile as I silently thank them too.

"I love you too, Trip, You're the only thing I will ever truly want for the rest of my life."

TRIP AND I HAVE NOT been able to stop being disgustingly loved up since the night in the park and it makes me smile so much my face hurts. It's been a few days and we both have to tone it down this afternoon so I can be introduced to some of his less legitimate business ventures. We are currently in his office with Luca discussing where I can fit in.

"I mean when we need to take someone out quietly, that's your department." Luca states.

"What about Paul, isn't that his job?" I ask,

"He will do it if we ask but he prefers the admin side, I am sure he would want to tag along from time to time but he would definitely prefer to take a backseat." Trip answers,

"Ok, anything else?" I look between them,

"We can include you on any group jobs, like when we need to talk down another up-and-coming gang, obviously you can help if another war between the families break out but neither of those are day to day." I nod in agreement.

"Look, I appreciate you guys trying to include me, but you can't just add me in somewhere, how about you treat me like a specialist you delegate jobs or issues to me when they come up, that way there's no pressure to make sure I have something to do and I can get on with my own work in between?"

"Works for me, Trip?"

"Ok, but I do want you to be more involved."

"Just give it time, you'll find stuff to delegate to me." I wink at Trip who raises an eyebrow at me. "Ok, so has anyone had any more ideas to find Jay?' Trip shakes his head; I look to Luca who looks unsure. "Out with it."

"He was working with the Cartel; I think he's with them."

"It makes sense, once my favour was repaid, they had no loyalty to me." Trip adds,

"So, we get in the cartel, we get answers, we get out?" I ask

"That would be the plan but this is the cartel they shoot first then realise they can't ask questions to corpses." Luca states,

"So, we go in, cause a bit of bloodshed, get answers from a survivor, then get out?" They both nod. "I will do some digging and then we can get a proper plan together."

<hr>

WHEN I AM SUMMONED from my HQ, I hate that name has actually stuck, I join the guys out the back where thousands of candles are lit, making it look like something off a rom com.

"What's going on?" I ask Paul as I step up beside him. He looks at me then smiles.

"Finally, Skye over here." I walk to where Tiago is looking very nervous. "So, I thought about proposing again, but I don't think I can handle another rejection, hence my fool proof plan."

"What fool proof plan?" He shoves a folded sheet of paper into my hand, "You're going to do it!" He states as he walks away further into the garden, I open my mouth to refuse but I am interrupted,

"Show time." Luca calls, as I turn around Trip is leading out a gasping Millie. Fuck me! Millie makes her way to me with confusion over her face,

I clear my throat and unfold the letter. I scan over the words and then screw the paper up.

"Millie, If I were into girls, I would have already proposed to you, however I seem to be into guys specifically a mafia boss with way too much money and muscles." She chuckles and so do the guys, "There is someone that is so in love with you he has already asked you to marry him but you stupidly said no, as your best friend it is my duty to fix the mistake, that man standing over In the garden behind me loves you so much he couldn't handle it if you said no again so he smartly got someone you can't refuse to ask you instead. Millie, you are the best person in this world, you are kind, you love with your whole heart and you are loyal to a fault, will you make me the happiest best friend to ever live and marry the dumbass so you can finally have the life you deserve?" A tear falls from her eye as she nods, then laughs then nods again. I pull her into a hug and I squeeze tight. "Go put him out of his misery." I let her go and as she walks over to Taio Trip hugs me from behind, his chin on my shoulder.

"This will be us one day."

"Not if you have a speech as bad as mine." I grin and he chuckles. We watch as Millie hugs Taio and the biggest smile stretches across his face, he gets on one knee then pulls out a ring box, her hand flies over her mouth before she gives it back to him so he can put the ring on her. Taio stands, grabs Millie and picks her up, spinning her around in the air. I can feel how happy they are from here and I feel the warm wet drops falling from my eyes as I watch them go into the next stage of their lives.

Chapter Twenty – Eight

"I have a meeting with Ricky in an hour and his answers will be the deciding factor on whether we go in on the Cartel." Trip says as he renters the bedroom part of the suite we have in Mexico.

"Can you trust him to tell the truth?" I ask,

"I can't, but he knows I know how to read him like a god damned book."

"Is it even worth tipping off the Cartel about why we are here?" Trip comes to me and wraps his arms around me,

"I think we should try anything that could reduce the amount of blood spilled."

"Ok, but I am coming with you."

"I didn't expect anything less, but you will be hidden from view. Ok?"

"Fine." I roll my eyes and Trip shakes his head, kissing me on the forehead which makes all sorts of warm fuzzies to escape into my chest.

I am currently lurking in the shadows, watching Trip as he waits for his guy to show, the other guys are on standby at the hotel, ready to meet us at the Cartels base if we call them in. If Jay is here or the Cartel have any information on where he is then this is our only shot to get anything amicably. Another car pulls into the wide-open space that's at the end of the dirt road, no one is coming here unless they up to their own shady shit. A man gets out of the car the same time Trip gets out of his, Trip looks confident and in control exuding the power he's accumulated by being a mafia boss, the other guy, Ricky, is fidgety and meek. I can feel his fear from here, what's he so scared of? He knows Trip, they get along and have been doing business together for years. I watch the conversation between the two and see when Trip's shoulders slump slightly and with a shake of his head I know we are going in hard. This guy with whatever he has said has told Trip all he needs to know. Trip turns towards his car to get in but Ricky doesn't move an inch, I notice another man pop up from the back seat of the car Ricky arrived in and pull a gun through the already open window aiming it at Trip, my own gun is out and aimed at the guy before I've even registered the action. Without thinking about it I pull the trigger and the guy is taken out instantly, Trip turns at the sound of gunfire and pulls his own gun. He takes a split second to evaluate the situation and then pulls his own gun and shoots Ricky between the eyes. I walk back to the car and get in the passenger side and Trip follows,

"Fucking hell!" Trip hits the steering wheel in frustration, "This just got a whole lot messier!"

"Why? And why were they trying to kill you?"

"The Cartel is working with another boss, one that hates me and has wanted my territory for a while, Ricky thought that's why I am here, they have a very lucrative deal happening with Francesco and part of the deal is to take me out."

"More reason to strike now then."

"Yes, but now we have to deal with him as well as Jay, we need to take one of the higher ups for questioning. Brief the others, we hit now." I take out my phone as Trip puts the car in drive and heads out. This is going to be a hell of a mission and I just pray we all make it out unharmed.

"THE SECURITY IS HIGH, but thing we can't handle, we need to be discreet, melee takedowns and hide bodies for as long as we can, we are severely out manned and we have to play this right to succeed. We have to get through to the inner ring of the compound that's where we can go all out-shoot to kill, Luca you are in charge of finding the one to keep alive and getting him out of the way while we dismantle the Cartel from the inside out." Paul hands out some earpieces to everyone and we all load up on bullets and strap as many knives and guns to our bodies as we can.

"We do this as quickly as we can, we spread out and conquer just like Paul said, this needs to go quietly and smoothly until we are in the inner circle. Stay low, stay unseen, stay alive." Trip demands and we all nod. Trip grab my wrist just as it run to walk away from the van with the others. "I know you would say no if I asked you to stay out of this, so instead I am going to kiss you like it's a normal day and force myself to allow you to walk in there." I smile and then he does as he says, his lips come down on mine and it's a heart meltingly sweet kiss. He squeezes me to him for a moment before letting go and walking away. I walk over to the back of the compound which takes a bit because the size of it is decent, staying in the shadows I join Luca and Taio.

"Taio, you hang back and take out anyone you see trying to escape or raise alarm, we will sweep the first few rings then you join us." Taio nods, "As Paul said earlier there are two doors to the outside, the front where he and Trip are going through and the back where we are, the inside layout is slightly different. Each ring will house 4 main doors that enter the next ring you will know these doors when you see them, to make our lives much easier the doors to any rooms are all on the outside walls and we want the doors on the inside. Choose a direction and stick with it even after you go through another door, that way we are all sweeping a fourth of each ring and everywhere has been completely covered."

"Got it, I'll take right you take left." I state and Luca nods.

"Now Luca has kindly ran through the plan again for no reason, can we gets started." Trip says in my ear,

"I was just making sure she knew; Skye has never worked with us before." I chuckle,

"It's because I am girl, isn't it?" I tease and Luca goes pale while Taio snorts a laugh.

"No, of course not..."

"Ok, we can finish this later, let's go." Paul's voice says in my ear, I turn to face the wall just in the distance and start running for it. Luca keeps level with me both of us staying in the shadows as much as possible. I run at the wall kicking off of the side using the momentum to run up the wall a few steps until I can grip the top of the stone and pull myself up, I quickly swing my legs to the other side and drop down, making sure my body stays limp and relaxed to prevent an injury from such a big drop. A few seconds later and Luca is next to me. We take our time closing in on the building, Luca stays hidden as he gets to the wall and cuts the cable for the sensor light, allowing me to literally stroll to the door.

"We are in position." I say,

"We are just approaching the door, hold out for another minute." Trip's voice again. "Ok in position, three, two, one."

Luca pulls the door open while I stand with my knife in my hand, no one is right by the door so we enter, I go right and Luca goes left as planned. I walk along the corridor for a few minutes before I see the first guard. His back is turned so on silent feet I approach him and before he is even aware I am there his neck is snapped and I guide his body to the floor. Where the fuck am I meant to hide the body, there's no rooms in this corridor! I say as much to the guys through the earpiece.

"Yeah, we are having this too, we thought there would maybe be a utility closet or guards office or something in this corridor, but nothing so unless you all want to walk these bodies back outside, we are going to have to leave them where they are." Luca states,

" I am already moving on." I say, It takes ten minutes and three guards in total to get to the next door, I am leaning against the wall when Trip approaches with a grin. "I chose right so you chose right?" I ask and his grin widens,

"Ready for the next door." He states for the others,

"In three." We all count down in our heads and enter, this time there is a small walkway from the door into the corridor, I am assuming the long walls on each side of me right now are for the rooms Luca mentioned. When we enter the actual corridor its empty like the last one, Trip smacks my arse before heading left. I roll my eyes, I check all the rooms and take out any men that are in them, also the one guard in the corridor, nothing to bad so far but we have one more corridor and the inner circle to go.

I TWIRL THE BLOODY blade in my palm as I approach Trip at the last door,

"You look like you're having fun," He cocks an eye, I shrug, I know I have a curve to the corner of my lip and a glint in my eye but I have to enjoy my job else I wouldn't do it right. I know I am not the same girl he met and there's this broken part of me that loves to take away the life of the sick evil people in this world and I probably always will now. I could argue that Trip is one of those people but he's a good bad, like me.

"Ready." I say with a wink to Trip.

"We have Taio, guns out and on three." Paul says, I wait pressed to the wall a gun in one hand a knife in the other for Trip to kick in the door, when he does, he retreats to the wall again. We take out anyone who comes into the corridor easily enough then side by side we walk into the inner circle. It's instant carnage when we enter, there are people everywhere guns being pulled and bullets flying through the air. I take out five guys in succession and keep my eyes out for any surprise attacks, I take my time and keep calm as people rush out of the rooms into the inner circle and more men fire at us. I fire my gun and hit my target, then repeat using my knife on anyone that gets to close aiming for the easy kill, the throat. We thin the crowd quickly and easily but we have at least sixty men to still get through, I go to one of the side rooms and clear it, upturning the desk for a little cover, bopping up and down taking a shot when I have one. I take too long reloading and one of them gets the jump on me, pouncing from over the desk, kicking me in the face causing my head to snap to the side, he's on top of me and is raining down punches, I use his momentum to roll us so I am on top of him an land a few punches of my own. I feel the pain in my face and use it to fuel my anger, the anger fuels my strength and with a grip on his neck I squeeze. His eyes go wide as his windpipe starts to crush under me, he can see the monster gleaming in my eyes at his impending death and all fight leaves him, his eyes slowly drain of light until they go glassy and I release my hold. I spit blood out of mouth next to the body and look up and over the edge of the desk, the crowd is much thinner now, the guys must have been constantly taking them out while I was fucking around with this guy. I stand and press myself against the wall by the door taking peeks around it to see what the situation is and any marks I can shoot from my position.

"Fuck, I am hit." Comes through the earpiece in a very pained voice,

"Where how bad?" Trip demands,

" Thigh, not too bad but we need to wrap this up quick." That's Luca's voice, I pop out from the wall and scan the room, I see him leaning against the wall in one of the hallways Leading into the main room. The others can't see him from their position and men are closing in on him. I reload my weapon and pull out another gun, with one in each hand I make my move, I run in to the centre of the room and of the action, killing everyone I come across, vaulting over furniture and leaping over bodies. I take down every man who was closing in on Luca, except the one who is grabbing him the way I would if I wanted to snap his neck. I drop a gun, the chances of hitting Luca too high and grab a knife, I don't think, I don't second guess, I throw. It sails through the air and hits its target in the throat, I get to them just as the man starts to lose his consciousness and rip the knife through him, Blood arcs in the air spraying me and Luca and it's a horrific scene, they guy drops to my feet and I smirk at Luca's shell shocked face.

"How's that for a girl?"

Chapter Twenty – Nine

The notification that someone's at the door of my HQ rings around me, and I press the button on my computer that allows access. Luca hobbles in and takes a seat next to me. Me and Luca came home while the others stayed to try and get information out of the one and only survivor. It's been a few days and Luca has now started to venture out of his bedroom with the aid of some crutches, his leg will be ok it just needs some time to heal, so he is not to put any pressure on that leg.

"Hey." I say while continuing to tap on the keyboard.

"Hey, you look busy."

"Just some recon work for a couple of jobs, you ok?"

"Yeah, the pains more of an annoyance than actual pain now, which is why I came down here." I look at him now and raise an eyebrow, he looks pensive and he is looking at the ground. "I wanted to thank you, if it weren't for you, I would have been dead long before the guys even figured out where I was."

"You don't need to thank me Luca, we stick together, and you would have done the same for any of them and me, right?"

"Yes, of course I would have. But I still want to thank you anyway, you saved me even though, none of us were there to save you."

"Is that what this is about, guilt over what Jay did?" He nods and I sigh, I turn to face him fully and take his hands in mine, he looks at me then and I smile. "I have come to realise that I am the only person who can really save myself from Jay, I could have saved myself from him years ago and it wouldn't have got as far as it did but then I wouldn't have you guys, I would still be all alone in the world, well, except from Millie. It had to happen how it did, do I wish he never got to me in Paris, of course I do, but if he didn't, he would have either been a shadow I would have been scared of for the rest of my life or he would have attacked at a different time. I have to finish this, no one else can do it for me, and don't ever feel guilt for what he did."

"We can help you."

"I know and you will, I will finish this once and for all and then my family will help me live my life without fear, you all will fill my life with adventure, love and joy. That's all I need." Luca smiles, "Come on, let's go get food."

MILLE HAS TAKEN OVER my bed with wedding magazines and a huge folder with all of her plans in, she's trying to take my mind off things, I have been stressed these past couple of days. Trip, Taio and Paul are all still in Mexico trying to extract information and the longer they're their the more anxious I get, plus they haven't gotten anything useful yet, I don't think they are going to either which leaves us one option to get to Jay.

"Do you think gold centre pieces are too tacky?" She asks pulling me out of my own head,

"I am not sure, why don't you hire a planner, surely they would be more help than me?"

"I just want it to be special, I think I should do it all."

"Millie. Come on, you're going to have the most special day no matter what but hiring someone to help is not pushing yourself out of the planning but allowing you to enjoy the process more because you won't be so stressed."

"Hmm,"

"Look, hire someone give them a two-week trial run and if you don't like the idea after that I will personally fire them."

"Fine." She starts putting everything away and stacking into a pile, I do spot the slight smile she tries to hide. The generic ringtone echoes around the room and I launch myself at the phone pressing answer as on as my fingers grip the device.

"Hello." I say,

"We're coming home," Trip's voice sounds tired and deflated,

"When?"

"We are boarding the jet in an hour."

"Are you ok?" I ask,

"We didn't get anything from him, I am so sorry Skye, It's another dead end."

"Hey, stop that! You have nothing to apologise for, you all did everything you could, so cheer the fuck up else you will have hell to pay when you finally get home." Trip chuckles and it makes me smile.

"I love you Skye, see you soon."

"I love you too." I throw the phone next to me on the bed and bury my face in my hands.

"So, what you going to do?" Millie asks,

"Plan b, I am going to be bait. "I lean back against the headboard of my bed,

"Can you not just forget about him, he's been in hiding for five years, I doubt he will risk coming after you again."

"I think he will, but we can prove your theory by me being bait, if he doesn't come, we will know for sure." She moves off the bed and glares at me from the end.

"How exactly are you going to be bait?"

"Three steps, and the first I need your help with like."

"Step two and three?"

"You'll see, are you going to help me or not?" Millie rolls her eyes, then nods. I get up from the bed and grab her arm pulling her into the bathroom.

I hear the guys before I see them, when they walk into the kitchen where I am nursing a coffee, Trip halts and makes the other two bump into him,

"Dude what's... oh." Taio says she looks around Trip to see me,

"Trip, you ok?" I ask before I sip my coffee.

"You look like you." He says and I laugh,

"I am me so that's a weird thing to say." I tease, the others move around a still shell-shocked Trip and grab their own coffees before taking seats, they're both smirking at Trip which makes me smile. I look back to Trip who now looks confused,

"Is it real?"

"Yes, it's real," I get up and push my long auburn curls over my shoulders, it now reaches the bottom of my back when curly so I have no idea how long it will be straight.

"How?" This one from Taio,

"Very patient hairdresser and a good wig." I answer and then the confusion is gone, Trip stalks towards me and runs his hands through my hair, his lips slamming onto mine in a passion filled kiss. I go onto my tip toes and curve my body into his, deepening the kiss. When he pulls away, I am breathless, he looks over my shoulder to the other guys then I see the glint of mischief in his eyes just before I am hauled over his shoulder and he walks out of the kitchen, Paul and Taio laughing as we go.

"Viola, hi!" I greet as I walk to the table Viola is currently waiting for me at, she stands, her face as beautiful as ever as her blonde hair swishes at her back in the sleek ponytail she has it styled in.

"Skye, mia cara, come stai, sono stato così preoccupato dopo quel terribile attacco." We both take a seat and I smile,

"Viola, I still don't speak any Italian." She laughs,

"How are you?"

"I am very well, thank you for asking, I saw your latest movie, you're doing ok too by what the box office is saying."

"Thank you, it is my favourite movie so far. I am doing well in my career, but enough about me, I do not want to hear anything other than your big comeback as a model!"

"And what Viola asks for she shall receive." I wiggle my eyebrows and she gasps her eccentric personality shining as always. "I want to make a big comeback, I am tired of hiding, and I thought who better to make it happen that's Viola and Camiellia."

"Yes, yes I will call her now, we will sort everything. You worry no more; this will be a worldwide comeback that will go down in history!"

"How about we eat first?"

"No! We have no time to waste." Viola gets up her face scrunched in concentration. "You are back with Trip, no?" I nod "I will arrange everything now, I will be in touch with all the details, you will see." And with that she rushes out of the door, I hold in my chuckle and now I remember why I liked her so much.

Chapter Thirty

I was looking forward to today when I woke up, after weeks of non-stop photo shoots, meetings, finding time for missions and helping Millie and her wedding planner create what seemed like the most fun, relaxed and elegant wedding event of the century. However, I am wound up like a spinning top and I am trying not to bite off the very expensive nails I had done yesterday. We are two hours away from walking down the aisle that's been set up in the gardens outside and Millie has kicked out all of the beauty team and locked herself in the bathroom. I could break the door down or pick the lock easy enough but I am letting her have her meltdown now, I thought it would take like thirty minutes max but it's been an hour and a half and I can still hear her crying through the door.

"Millie?"

"Go away!" She shouts, I think about calling one of the guys to help me out here, but I am her best friend I should know how to fix this, right?

"Ok, Millie, I just want you to hear me out, once I've spoken I will leave if you still want that." I wait for a response and continue when there isn't one. "You are my best friend, I love you and I will back you with whatever you want or need no matter what, so if you want me to get you out of here, I have a fake passport with your name on it and cash in a suitcase. No one will ever find us we can go if you want, but I think you should stay and marry the love of your life. Taio is amazing and he's also amazing to you, cold feet is normal but talk to me, lets air it all out and make a decision. Crying alone in the bathroom as your wedding guests arrive is not the greatest plan." I move away from the door and attempt to wait patiently sitting on the bed, after what feels like an eternity, the lock clicks and Millie comes and sits beside me.

"I love him so much it hurts and I love thinking of our future an how happy we would be, but then I think of his role in the mafia and what that would look like as our kids grow up, our kids would be trained and moulded to take positions like the guys and they will have to see so much bad that they might lose all their goodness, they might become monsters like Jay." I stare at her wide eyed.

"You have nothing to worry about, look at us, look at the guys. Have we all lost the good inside of us? Ok we are not stellar human beings but we aren't evil. We have a family that love us and morals which will all be handed down to our kids, yes, they may be taught to shoot as well as how to ride a bike, especially if we have any girls but that won't make them any less amazing. Your kids will be kind and decent always because you are their mum and you are the best human that any of us know. Plus, Rina will make sure they are respectable and decent."

"You promise?"

"I do, I will kick their arses if they start straying." She chuckles,

"You're going to be an amazing mum too,"

"Auntie first, we will work up to parenthood, ok?" She nods, "Can we please get the beauty team back in and get back on track now?" She laughs and nods again, I hug her tightly, "I will always have your back."

"I know."

Two hours and four glasses of champagne later and I am walking my best friend down the aisle, Taio is standing at the end waiting for her with a tear in his eye. Luca is standing proud next to him, then there's Trip who is staring at me with a hopeful look on his face and finally Paul who is ordaining the wedding. When we reach the end of the aisle, I hug her tightly and take her hand placing it in Taio's before taking my place next to her.

"We have come together today to witness the marriage of two very special people, Taio and Millie. We have watched them over the years grow as people and as a couple and it is my honour to take them through this ceremony which will bind them as husband and wife for the rest of their days. Before we start, I do have to ask if there are any objections to this wedding, but I will warn you to look at the groomsmen before any objections are made and just think about if their wrath is worth it." The three glare at the audience and some who are within the mafia let out small chuckles. "Good, The couple have chosen to forgo any long vows as they wish to do this in private, so we are going to skip to the main ones. Taio Murino, do you take this woman, Millie Darrington to be your lawful wedded wife? To love and respect her? In sickness and in health? For as long as you both shall live?"

"I do." Taio's voice breaks a bit but his smile shows how happy he is, he takes the ring from his brother and slides it on to Millie's finger.

"Millie Darrington, do you take this Man, Taio Murino to be your lawful wedded husband? To love and respect him? In sickness and in health? For as long as you both shall live?"

"I do." I hand her the ring and she smiles before turning back around, she slides the ring on his finger effortlessly.

"With the powers vested in me, I pronounce you husband and wife and you may now kiss the bride." Everyone claps and cheers as they kiss, they turn and hand in hand walk back down the aisle. Trip comes to me taking my arm in his and walks me down the aisle too.

"You look beautiful." He whispers in my ear,

"You're not so bad yourself." I smirk,

"We could sneak away for a while, no one would notice."

"Stop, no we can't, we have an hour of photos, then the sit-down dinner then the reception." Trip pouts adorably.

"You can get me drunk, spin me around the dance floor then take me to bed." I waggle my eyebrows.

"I don't think I have ever seen you drunk, how about we sneak off at some point get that out the way, then we can both get drunk, dance like idiots and pass out later."

"I like your plan." We both smile at each other, tonight's going to be a great night.

I wake up the next morning feeling ready to throw up, we definitely got wasted last night, my head is pounding and my mouth is dryer than the Sahara desert. I peel my eyes open to see Millie's face next to mine, her wedding dress still on. What the fuck happened last night. I fight through the hangover gravity weighing my body down and slowly sit up, I take in the sight and smile, cuddled together at the end of the bed are Trip and Taio, I nudge Millie and she groans so I shh her, she opens one eye and takes in my grin, I point to our men and she lifts her head to look, she barks out a laugh and I groan as it hurts my head.

"Do you remember how we ended up here, all together?"

"No, we drank way too much, I do remember us racing to see who could chug a bottle of champagne first then it's all fuzzy."

"Not our best idea."

"No it was not." Luca's voice fills the room from beside me, I look for him but I can't see him, I look over the side of the bed and giggle at his form on the floor.

"Huh, so only Paul was sensible then."

"No, I am here!" A hand shoots up from Millie's side of the bed and Millie starts laughing and soon I am joining in.

"What, dude get off me." Taio says, pushing Trip, who was spooning him, away. Trip lands on the floor with a grunt and it makes our laughing fit even worse. When we have wiped the tears from our eyes and calmed down, Millie asks,

"What the hell happened last night?"

"Your best friend stole you, kept on saying she's mine, she was mine first I have dibs." Taio states with a pout.

"Oh, well she has a point." Millie smiles and I shrug, putting my arm over her shoulder.

"Don't be jealous, you got to put a ring on it." I tease.

"Besides, looks like Trip kept you company." Millie says with a waggle of her brows and I snort a laugh.

"He's a good big spoon, bet he kept you snuggled all night." Trip pops up with a grin,

"Yeah man, I made sure you weren't cold and lonely on your wedding night, and what thanks do I get huh, I get pushed off the bed!"

"Your so mean, Taio." I add. Trip comes to sit next to me and he winks at me.

"Your all dickheads!" Taio grumbles as he crawls up the bed to plonk his head on Millie's stomach, she runs her fingers through his hair. I lean on Trip and he hugs me too him, before I know it, we are all back asleep at least this time cuddling the right partners.

We arrive In London a few days after the wedding and seeing all the familiar streets as we drove past was weird, I always thought a part of me missed my hometown but actually I could never set foot here again and not think twice about it. Trip is pacing behind me as I have my makeup done, he hates this plan and has made his opinion known a lot over the last twenty-four hours.

"Surely there's a way for one of us to come with you." He muses, I nod to the makeup artist who smiles and leaves us,

"No, we have been over this, I have to go to the event alone and then I go to the other hotel, if he sees any of you he may not show, and I need this over."

"I can wait at the other hotel, hide in the suite, you should have some back up!" I stand and face him.

"Trip! You need to trust that I can do this on my own, I have to do this on my own." His solder sag as he sits on the bed and runs his hands sown his face.

"I know, I just hate the thought of you getting hurt."

"Jay has no idea of what I have done or become over the last five years and he will not be expecting for me to be able to fight back. He thinks he's preying on the girl who used to cower in the corner, not the woman who can and will kill him with her bare hands." I stand in between his legs and up his face bringing his eyes up too meet mine. "This time I am the monster and I will be the better one." I kiss him gently, pouring my feelings for him into it before ripping myself from him and heading out the door.

Chapter Thirty – One

I bite my nails as I ride the lift up to my suite, the event was awful, I thought I saw Jay out of the corner of my eye every time I turned my head and the fear I had for him keeps trying to creep up within me, I have to stay calm, focused and lethal for me to get the upper hand, I can't lose this fight. What would have been the point of everything, of enduring the pain from him, of loving Trip, of making my family, of becoming a monster just to fail now? My chance to finally be completely free and too live how I want to live is tonight, I have no doubt that Jay will show, that's just who he is. He wouldn't be able to stand seeing me in those magazines looking healthy and happy, he would have known about tonight's event as we made sure everyone would know I would be there giving him the perfect opportunity to finish me off for good. The lift dings as I reach my floor and after a deep claiming breath, I hold my head up high and enter the suite I turn the lights on and as expected, my nightmare lounges on the sofa with a nasty smirk on his lips.

"Well, look who it is? Dresses like a well-paid whore I see."

"Jay, what, how are you here?" I act scared, not wanting him to suspect the trap.

"You really are a dumb bitch! Do you think you can strut around having the time of your life and I wouldn't find you? Especially after you put your fat arse in all of those magazines!" He stands and takes two steps towards me?

"I just want to get on with my life, I haven't done anything to you. Why can't you just leave me alone?"

"You lying slut! Done nothing to me? You ruined me! I have had to hide in a shithole for five years because of you, my life was put on pause the day you opened your big mouth on tv!" His fists clench at his side, the rage in his eyes makes me want to flinch but I remind myself I am stronger now.

"You did all of those things to yourself, none of what I said was a lie, you beat me, sold me, and faked my death! Then you tried to kill me! You ruined your own life by trying to end mine, you only have yourself to blame." I seethe.

"If it weren't for you fucking him, I would be rolling in money and living g the life I deserve!" He practically screams before launching himself at me. I freeze for a split second but thankfully muscle memory kicks in and I dodge his fist spinning and kicking him in the back making him crash to the floor. I let pure anger take over me and I waste no time in getting to him, I grab his hair in my fist and smash his face onto the floor three times before he gets some leverage under him and rolls over breaking my hold. He jumps up and wipes the blood that's streaming down his face from his eyebrow and nose. Jay comes at me again, this time I don't move quick enough and he clips my jaw causing my head to snap to the side, he kicks the back of my leg causing me to go down on one knee, I don't allow him to do more, I punch him in the dick and his pained groan brings me too much joy for me to be sane. I stand quickly and stop playing defence, I attack punching him in quick succession, some in the face and some in the side. I land a kick to his chest and the force of it sends him flying backwards and sliding across the floor, I am on him before he can recover, straddling his waist as I rain down blow after blow to his face. I see his eyes start to roll back,

"You are not passing out; you will watch as I finish this!" I growl, his eyes widen unnaturally when my hands grip his throat tight,

"Please, Skye! I am sorry, please." He begs, his nails scratch my arms but I ignore the sharp pain and the lines of blood forming on my skin. I feel a tear escape my eye, it's not out of sadness, its anger, anger for how he treated me, for every bruise he put on me, for the scar on my face and for the trauma I will always carry. How dare he beg me to stop, he laughed when I pleaded for him not to hurt me, he enjoyed leaving me physically and mentally broken, my grip tightens with that thought.

"I will never forgive you," I spit. I watch the life leave his eyes, I slump to the floor beside his corpse and breathe deeply, in and out, in and out. I won. I finally fucking won. After a while I get to my feet and leave with my head held high and never looking back.

Trip's gaze snaps to me as soon as I lose the door, he takes in my body looking for injury, I know he sees all the blood on me, the bruise forming on my jaw and the cuts from on my arms.

"It's mostly his," I say waving my hand over me, Trip nods before grabbing me and pulling me into his embrace, I can feel how tense he is and the any he's holding on to me so tightly tells me how worried he was. "I am good Trip, I did it, it's over." I feel him shudder and I look up to his face, his eyes are glossy as if he is holding back tears. I feel his hand on my face and I lean into his warm touch,

"It's over." He whispers, like he needed to say it to make it real. I smile up at him.

"Once I am showered, he's gone forever."

"I can help with that." Trip states and he grabs my wrist hauling me behind him, once we are in the bathroom, he turns on the shower and checks the temperature while I shut the door. Trip gently removes my dress, shoes and underwear then lifts me by my waist and puts me under the spray, he quickly strips himself and joins me. The water is hot but feels so good beating down on my skin, Trip takes the sponge and pours shower gel on it before running it over every inch of my body making sure my skin is thoroughly cleaned. I stare at his face the whole time he does this, ignoring the tingles on my skin every time his skin touches me, and I know I have found true love, I found a love that will last forever and no matter what happens will never dim. I will love this man for the rest of my life and even after and all I want to do I live everyday with him.

"Marry me?" I blurt, his hands freeze in place and his gaze locks with mine,

"What?" He asks his eyebrows furrowing,

"I want to be tied to you in every possible way for the rest of my life, I want to be your wife, the mother of your children and I want to be with you every day until I die. So, marry me?" After an agonising second or two a smile breaks out on his face and he leans down to kiss me, it's slow but it's the only answer I need.

Epilogue

Two years later.

I am woken up by an insane amount of pressure in my bladder, I groan as I swing my legs over the bed and slowly stand, I am two weeks away from my due date and I am massive, I start to waddle towards the bathroom when the pressure suddenly goes, I feel the water flood down my legs and a puddle quickly appears around my feet. "Oh shit!"

"Skye?" Trip asks sleepily,

"Trip, it's time." Trip rolls over and looks at something on his bedside table,

"It's three twenty-five, come back to bed."

"Not what's the time, It's time, ahh fuck." I groan as a pain radiates across my back and then over my protruding belly. Trip rolls out of bed and rushes to my side, the look of pure horror on his face.

"It's time, shit! It's time." He runs out of the bedroom and starts shouting around the house. I tune him out, grab the sweats, and top I've had waiting by the bathroom for weeks. I put my hair in a bun and have the quickest shower before getting out and getting dressed. Breathless I sit on the toilet and cringe as another contraction hits.

"Skye?" Millie shouts from the bedroom,

"In here." Millie opens the door and pops her head into the room,

"Should I tell them to get the car?" I nod and she smiles. I hear her retreat from the bedroom then command the guys to get the car and the bags. She returns to me and grabs my hands helping me back to my feet. "Everything's going to be fine, we will get you set up at the hospital and in a few hours it will all be over." I nod, she knows how scared I've been about the labour, we walk out of the bedroom and pause as I have a contraction then continue downstairs, they guys are all in a panic, running back and forth not knowing what they are actually doing.

"So much for drilling the plan into their heads." I grumble,

"Taio get the baby bag." Trip commands and Taio trips up the stairs as he rushes to do what he's told.

"Paul the car!" Trip shouts, I walk to the kitchen where Rina is waiting with a mug of hot chocolate for me.

"Here, you relax, they will figure it out soon enough."

"Are all men this frantic when a woman goes into labour?" Millie asks with an eye roll and Rina just nods with a chuckle,

"This is where men are the most stupid." I cry out in pain as the contraction worsens,

"For fuck's sake, sort yourselves out, your only job is to get the bags and the car! There's four of you, figure it out!" Millie growls, I look to the doorway of the kitchen where Trip and Luca are putting their guns away, if I weren't in pain I would laugh. I take a sip of my drink and then we hear the beep of the car, the guy's rush to it and Millie takes my arm as we walk to the front door. As we get to the threshold, we see the car speeding down the long drive, I look Millie in shock and she returns the expression.

"I am going to fucking kill them!" I grumble, We watch as the car almost reaches the gates before making a u turn and heading right back, Trip falls out the car and runs to me,

"I am so fucking sorry," He says as he helps me walk,

"You are all fucking dead when I am done giving birth!"

"I know, we are sorry, come on let's get you to the hospital."

I AM SET UP IN A REALLY nice room, Millie and Trip are on each side of the bed and it would be nice, if this didn't hurt like a fucking bitch.

"Baby, please don't cry." Trip says as he runs his fingers through my hair, I push him away,

"You! You did this to me!" His face pales and he looks so guilty, I cry harder, "I am sorry, come back." He comes back to me and slips his hand in mine; the next contraction hits and he hisses as I squeeze his hand. "Please can I push now?" I sob and the midwife checks me again,

"Ok, you're old to go." She grabs a stool and wheels it to the end of the bed where my legs are up and covered by a sheet. "When the contraction starts you dig deep and push, you stop pushing when the contraction ends." I nod, Millie pats my head with the cool we towel she has and her smile helps ground me. The contraction comes and with a growl I push with everything in me, when the contractions stop, I lean back,

"Trip I am so tired." I whine, he kisses my forehead,

"I know baby, but not much more now, I promise." I have never seen Trip look so helpless than right now. After two more contractions I decide I am not in the right position, I scoot forward,

"Trip get behind me." He climbs over the bed and I lean back against his chest, another contraction hits and I lean forward as I push with everything I have. Trip rubs my back and it helps a little, not much though.

"The heads out, one more push." The midwife states, it doesn't take long until the next contraction hits me and I feel better instantly when I hear my baby's little cry. The midwife hands the baby off to the doctor to get back into place.

"Ready for number two, this one is always the easier baby."

I wake up to Trip standing over my two babies, watching them while they sleep.

"Are they ok?" I ask groggily,

"They are perfect, just like their Mommy!" He says as he comes to me and kisses my forehead.

"Where is everyone?"

"I told them they had to wait until you had rested."

"So, the guys haven't met them? That's ridiculous, bring them in now!" I demand and Trip does as he's told. Luca and Taio rush in the room and beeline for the babies' cribs, Paul comes to me and kisses me on the cheek.

"Do you not want to see your niece and nephew?" I ask and he smiles,

"I do but I wanted to check in with you first, there's enough uncles that we can check on everyone." He states with a grin.

"I am good, go meet them!" I smile. Millie comes to me and chuckles at the guys who are just staring into the cribs looking lost.

"They are already wrapped around their tiny fingers." Mille says and I chuckle,

"I couldn't have wished for a better family for them." Mille smile is big and beaming, she nods before heading over to the guys,

"Ok, move Auntie Millie needs a cuddle!" They watch intently as she picks one of the babies up, taking mental notes of how to hold them, Trip gets the other baby and hands him to me.

"So? What are their names?" I grin as I cradle the most perfect little boy.

"This one is Jove and our princess is Jupiter."

Epilogue Two

"Jove? Jupiter? Where could they be?" I hear the two chuckles and pretend to look under the sofa even though they are behind the curtain,

"Babe, we need to go!" Trip says as he leans against the doorway of the living room,

"I know but I can't leave with kissing my babies and I can't find them anywhere." I say dramatically, there's more chuckles and Trip's eyes sparkle with humour.

"Should I activate the Daddy homing beacon?"

"Yes, they can't hide from that!"

"Beep, beep, beep." Trip makes his way towards the curtains and when he gets there, he rips it back revealing my two five-year-olds huddled together with huge grins. They pounce on Trip, climbing up him like monkeys and he walks them to me. I kiss each one and tell them how much I love them before handing them over to Millie and Taio.

"We can go now."

"Oh good." Trip sarcastically remarks and I roll my eyes,

"Hey! I am doing you a favour, remember?" Trip grabs my case off the floor and takes my hand as we walk to the car. I put my shades on and lean against the door, Trip puts the case in the boot and comes back to me, leaning down to kiss me briefly. His fingers play with the ends of my short blonde hair,

"Let's show Francesco what happens when you mess with Ruby Reapers husband." I laugh,

"After this Ruby is staying away for a while, we have a vacation to enjoy."

"I can't wait, three whole weeks with our family on the beach relaxing."

"I am not sure how much we can actually relax with Jove and Jupiter; they never stop."

"I can relax knowing that my family are together and extremely happy,"

"You're so sappy, what happened to you?" I tease,

"You did, you entered my life and changed everything. You make me happier every single day and words can't portray how much I fucking love you."

"I love you too, until the end of time." Trip smiles,

"Until the end of time and more." He kisses me again and I think of how we live our lives, it's not normal, it's not good or bad, but we are happy and most of all we are free to be who we are and no one can touch us.

Don't miss out!

Visit the website below and you can sign up to receive emails whenever K.L Hart publishes a new book. There's no charge and no obligation.

https://books2read.com/r/B-A-YXKU-HQMBC

BOOKS 2 READ

Connecting independent readers to independent writers.

Also by K.L Hart

Inheriting a Mafia
Inheriting a Mafia

The Divine Academy
The Divine Academy

The Knights of Knightingale Prep
Becoming a Knight

Standalone
The Better Monster

About the Author

About The Author

K.L Hart is the Author of The Storm Legacy series and The Divine Academy, she writes novels that are Young/New adult and most of her works have a dark sub story or background!

Get in touch!

social media

Instagram: www.instagram.com/Kerrylhart

Twitter:@kerry1hart

Kerrylhart92@gmail.com